"Good afternoon, ladies," he said, announcing himself with a straight face. "Did I hear my name mentioned?"

Zara spun on her heel, her expression impressively innocent considering how she'd just been gossiping about him. "You're a doctor here?"

"A locum. That's right." Conrad smiled, holding her gaze so she knew he'd overheard her comments. "But perhaps you don't recognize me with my clothes on?"

"You couldn't have mentioned that you're a doctor or that you work at *my* hospital the other morning?" she said, straight on the attack as she grabbed one of the ward tablets from the charging station and glared his way.

"I had planned on bringing it up when you mentioned shift work," he said, his lips twitching as he glanced down from her green-brown eyes to where she clutched the device the way she'd gripped that candlestick—with malicious intent. "But my fight-or-flight response got in the way. You looked menacing wielding that candlestick. And as you've seen me naked, I think it's only appropriate you call me Conrad, don't you?" He held out his hand in greeting, aware that the other two midwives were now frozen with awe and shamelessly eavesdropping.

Dear Reader,

I hope you enjoy Zara and Conrad's story. It was super fun playing around with these two opposites, who turned out to have plenty in common, especially their sense of humor! I loved the way sexy Australian Conrad brought Zara out of her shell. And midwife and mom Zara is such a caring and compassionate heroine. She easily saw through Conrad's armor to the vulnerabilities he was hiding underneath. The obstetric ward setting meant these two lovers could work together to deliver lots of babies. What could be more romantic?

Love,

JC x

THE MIDWIFE'S SECRET FLING

JC HARROWAY

MEDICAL ROMANCE

Harlequin®
MEDICAL
ROMANCE

Recycling programs
for this product may
not exist in your area.

ISBN-13: 978-1-335-94277-7

The Midwife's Secret Fling

Harlequin Enterprises ULC
22 Adelaide St. West, 41st Floor
Toronto, Ontario M5H 4E3, Canada
www.Harlequin.com

Printed in U.S.A.

Lifelong romance addict **JC Harroway** took a break from her career as a junior doctor to raise a family and found her calling as a Harlequin author instead. She now lives in New Zealand and finds that writing feeds her very real obsession with happy endings and the endorphin rush they create. You can follow her at jcharroway.com and on Facebook, X and Instagram.

Books by JC Harroway

Harlequin Medical Romance

A Sydney Central Reunion

Phoebe's Baby Bombshell

Buenos Aires Docs

Secretly Dating the Baby Doc

Gulf Harbour ER

Tempted by the Rebel Surgeon
Breaking the Single Mom's Rules

Forbidden Fling with Dr. Right
How to Resist the Single Dad
Her Secret Valentine's Baby
Nurse's Secret Royal Fling
Forbidden Fiji Nights with Her Rival

Visit the Author Profile page
at Harlequin.com for more titles.

To my mum.

**Praise for
JC Harroway**

"JC Harroway has firmly cemented her place as
one of my favourite Harlequin Medical Romance
authors with her second book in the imprint and with
wonderful characters and a heart-melting and very
sexy romance set in the beautiful Cotswolds."
—*Goodreads* on *How to Resist the Single Dad*

CHAPTER ONE

EARLY BOXING DAY MORNING, Zara Wood parked her car and left the cosy interior for the sub-zero temperatures outside. Craving a hot shower and a decadent five hours of uninterrupted sleep after her night shift at the hospital delivering babies, she pushed open the front gate to her Derbyshire cottage.

This early, the village of Morholme was quiet as people slept off the excesses of Christmas Day. Zara sighed; no matter which way she looked at it, working on Christmas night had sounded desperately lonely. But unless she counted watching her five-year-old son, Zach, sleep, something she still enjoyed, she'd had nothing better to do. Besides, most of the other midwives had families and partners, and Zach had been so excited for a sleepover at her mum's, where he'd no doubt eaten too many treats and stayed up late.

As she headed for the front door of the end-of-terrace cottage she'd inherited from her late father, a noise—the metallic scrape of the squeaky side gate—grabbed her attention.

Zara peered around the side of the house to see a strange woman disappear down the lane that ran between Zara's cottage and that of her neighbour. Zara raced into the garden, confusion turning to panic. Had she been burgled while she'd been at work? She'd spent six months renovating the basement rental flat while also working full-time to support her son single-handedly. Had the stranger broken in using the key Zara had hidden under a flowerpot for her new lodger— a man visiting from Australia—who was due later today?

With adrenaline ramping up her pulse, Zara yanked open the gate, outraged that someone had taken advantage of all her hard work. But by the time she'd made it into the lane, the woman had vanished.

Indignant, she entered the rental with her master key, fearful she'd find the lovely cosy accommodation she'd slaved over on her days off while Zach was at school completely ransacked, but everything appeared undisturbed. Even the television and portable speaker, the only items of real value, were still present. Perhaps the woman wasn't a thief at all, but a squatter.

Zara sighed, her five hours of sleep dissolving. She'd need to wait up for a locksmith to change the locks. Her mood worsened as she moved to the bedroom, finding evidence that the squatter had indeed spent the night. The bed Zara had left immaculately made for her lodger with clean luxury sheets and a cosy duvet was all rumpled and had obviously been slept in.

Just then, she caught the sound of the shower door closing in the en-suite bathroom. Her pulse soared. There were two squatters. And one of them was using *her* hot water and *her* luxury body wash. The cheek of people!

Melodic humming came from behind the closed bathroom door. *Male* humming. With a sudden chill of fear spreading through her veins, Zara grabbed the nearest heavy object—a ceramic candlestick from the mantel. She should probably call the police, but first, this guy was going to get a piece of her mind.

The bathroom door flew open. A stark-naked man appeared. On seeing Zara, he came to an abrupt halt in the doorway, his expression registering shock, which quickly morphed into a hesitant smile.

'I come in peace,' he said, holding up his hands in surrender as he nervously eyed the candlestick she'd menacingly raised. 'But if you're going to use that, do you mind if I cover myself first?' His eyes darted to the nearby towel rack.

'You can't be here,' Zara said, too strung out to

place his accent, but it was clear he wasn't local. She yanked an expensive Egyptian-cotton towel from the rail and tossed it at his naked chest.

He caught it with one hand and quickly wrapped it around his hips. 'Why don't you put down the candlestick before someone gets hurt?' he said, one side of his mouth kicking up, a playful edge to the nervousness now.

'There's nothing funny about breaking and entering,' Zara said, inflamed that he seemed to find this situation amusing. 'You're trespassing. If you don't leave immediately, I'll call the police.'

How dared these people take advantage of all her hard work? Renting out the newly finished flat would help subsidise her wages so she could give Zach everything he deserved in life, given that she'd never received a single penny of support from his father, a man Zara considered the biggest mistake of her life.

He held up his hands again now that the towel was securely tucked. 'Hey, there's no need for the police,' he said, as if she were overreacting. 'Let's just chill out for a second.'

'No, you chill out,' she volleyed back. 'And while you're at it, get out.' Thanks to this freeloader and his lady friend, she'd have to spend valuable time that she could have been sleeping fixing up the flat for the arrival of her lodger.

'I'm not trespassing,' the stranger said with amused patience, his inquisitive stare taking in Zara's creased midwife's uniform. 'Are you Mrs Wood? I'm Conrad Reed.'

At the mention of his name, Zara sagged with relief, her adrenaline draining away.

'It's *Ms* Wood, actually. I'm not married,' she snapped, feeling stupid. 'So you're Conrad Reed…from Australia?' There'd be no need to use the candlestick, call the police or change the locks, because *this* was her lodger, the man who'd signed a month-long lease and was supposed to be arriving that afternoon.

'Yep,' he said, his smile widening as he stuck out his hand. 'Good to meet you. If I'd known you were going to let yourself in, I'd have put on some clothes.' Humour flashed in his eyes.

Reluctantly, she shook his hand, her face flaming at the misunderstanding. But was everything a joke to this guy? Perhaps Aussies were just naturally easy-going thanks to all that sunshine and surfing. His accent was so obvious to her now, she cringed at her eagerness to jump to the wrong conclusion.

'Sorry,' she muttered. 'I thought you were a thief, or a squatter.' She lowered the candlestick to her side.

'Nope. But you weren't really going to use

that, were you?' He eyed her makeshift weapon doubtfully.

'I don't know...' She narrowed her eyes and stood a little taller. 'Maybe.'

He laughed then, but she couldn't join in or see the funny side. She was too tired.

'I hadn't thought it all the way through,' she continued. 'I just know that I worked hard to single-handedly renovate this place, and I've just got home from work after a night shift, and I have to pick up my son in five and a half hours so I was looking forward to some sleep and—'

She took a breath; she was waffling. This man didn't need her sad life story. And now that there was no need to evict him, she couldn't help but notice his attractiveness. Dirty-blond hair still damp from the shower. Piercing grey eyes, sparking with amusement. Tall and tanned with a muscular physique, his broad chest dotted with water droplets. Helpfully, her brain chose that moment to remind her that she'd seen him naked, even if she'd been too scared and outraged to enjoy it at the time.

But Conrad Reed's smokin' body and roguish good looks were irrelevant. Since a holiday fling six years ago had resulted in her precious baby, and after Zach's biological father had declared he wanted nothing to do with Zara or his son, her sole focus was taking care of Zach so he never once felt the loss of a positive male role model in his life. What with her shift work and her five-year-old, there was no energy left for members of the opposite sex, not even an exotic one with a drool-worthy body and a charming smile that came far too easily and made her think of all the things she'd denied herself since that pregnancy test had turned positive—partying, dates, *sex*.

'Hold on a second... You were meant to be arriving later this afternoon?' she reminded him, her voice pinched with fresh annoyance. She hoped her very first lodger, as hot as he was, wasn't going to be problematic.

'Change of plan. I took an earlier flight.' He gave a casual shrug, one hand pushing his wet hair back from his handsome face so his biceps bulged.

Zara grew hot, all too aware that it had been almost six years since she'd been intimate with a man, and that, but for her Egyptian-cotton towel and a cheeky grin, he was stark naked and impressively endowed.

'I did message late last night to let you know I'd arrived,' he said. 'Thanks for leaving out the key, by the way.'

'I don't check my phone when I'm working,' she said tightly, desperate to get away from his male confidence and amused curiosity. He was making her feel like an ancient, uptight freak.

'So is it too soon to joke about this yet?' he asked, flashing her the kind of smile that had probably rescued him from many a tricky situation. 'It's one hell of an introduction story.'

Zara raised her chin, feeling foolish for her part in the misunderstanding. 'Yes, I'm afraid it is.' He, on the other hand, seemed to find everything amusing. 'I'll…let you get dressed,' she said, wishing he were wearing more than a towel, his tall, lean body tauntingly on display.

She flushed hard. She was clearly exhausted; she wouldn't normally be susceptible to a guy's sexy confidence and charming smile. She turned for the bedroom door and then froze. The rumpled bed, the steamy bathroom, his freshly showered appearance finally registered, the pieces falling into place. Obviously her new laid-back lodger had entertained female company last night, and the mystery woman sneaking out of the side gate had not long left his bed. Or, more correctly, *Zara's* bed. Ignoring the sudden flare of irrational loneliness—her own nocturnal activities were non-existent by choice, despite her friend Sharon's constant urging she *have a little fun*—she fisted her hands on her hips and spun to confront him once more.

Having clocked the name badge on her uniform, Conrad had been about to mention that he'd taken a locum position at the same hospital, when she spun around, her lush mouth pursed with suspicion.

'Wait…' She frowned, her big hazel eyes taking another sweep of his naked torso before she met his stare. 'I just saw a woman leave here, but the lease was for you alone. Single occupancy.'

She looked embarrassed to mention it, but clearly wasn't scared of a little confrontation. And she clearly hadn't finished confronting him. At least she hadn't decked him with that heavy-looking candlestick…

'It *is* just me. Don't worry, she won't be back.' Conrad shrugged. What was a single doctor a long way from home supposed to do?

She flicked a glance at the unmade bed, her lip curling with disapproval as she slowly nodded. 'Oh, I see… So that woman isn't your girlfriend?'

Her stare returned to his, and then shifted over his chest. Ever since she'd decided he posed no threat, she couldn't seem to stop checking him out. And the curiosity, the attraction, was mutual. Zara Wood was a complete bombshell—petite, brunette, her body boasting the kind of curves that made him think of bikinis.

'Nah.' He shook his head, not in the slightest bit embarrassed to have been caught in the act of the morning after. 'I met her on the train. She gave me a lift from the station. It was just a one-time thing. No big deal.'

But from the way his feisty landlady was looking at him, he could tell she wasn't impressed.

'A one-night stand on your first night in town,' she said with a disbelieving slight shake of her head. 'Impressively fast work.'

Conrad smiled wider, wondering exactly what her problem was. She was only in her twenties, too young to be a prude. She had a son. Surely she must have had a one-night stand before.

'Is that not allowed?' he asked, fascinated by her prickly attitude. 'I don't recall anything in the lease agreement I signed that prohibits your tenants from having casual sex.'

'No problem at all,' she said, flushing but raising her chin defiantly. 'You can have as much casual sex as you like as far as I'm concerned. Who am I to judge?'

Conrad folded his arms over his chest, chuckling to himself when her stare dipped there once more. 'And yet you sound as if you're judging.'

His curiosity sharpened. Who was this intriguing woman and why was she so…uptight? He could understand the whole intruder misunderstanding, but she was acting as if she'd never once let her hair down.

'I'm not,' she bluffed haughtily. 'Your sex life

is none of my business.' She blushed furiously, looking away.

'Well, I'm glad we've got that cleared up.' Conrad nodded, smiling to himself.

'However…' Zara thrust the candlestick at him, so he took it with an incredulous snort of amusement. 'I do have a small son, so, as your landlady, I'd appreciate it if your, um…*guests* could limit themselves to your half of the garden.' She backed away towards the bedroom door as she spoke, as if she couldn't wait to get away from him now that she had him pegged as some sort of player.

'Of course, no worries,' he said with a shrug and a non-threatening smile. 'With this weather—' he glanced pointedly at the window and the grey skies beyond '—I don't think it will be an issue. It's hardly barbecue season. But I'll be sure to let you know of anyone else sleeping over. I don't want my *guests* bludgeoned in their sleep.' He held up the candlestick, his lips twitching with amusement. She was fascinating, formidable and so sexy.

'There's no need for that,' she said, appalled, the pitch of her voice rising. 'I don't need to know every time you have casual sex.'

'Are you sure?' he teased, unable to resist coaxing out the fiery sparks of challenge from her eyes. 'It's no problem to flick you a message.'

He should stop antagonising her and let her get some sleep, but, for some reason, he really wanted to see her smile.

'I'm positive, thanks.' The smile she offered him was frustratingly tight and insincere. Then she glanced down and muttered, 'I don't want to be inundated with messages.'

'What's that supposed to mean?' he asked, his stare narrowing. For someone with a son and no husband, she was acting fairly high and mighty. She'd obviously made some snap judgements about him, when all he'd actually done was arrive at a property he'd legally rented half a day early. Perhaps he and his landlady weren't going to get along after all. Shame, given they were most likely going to be work colleagues. But he wouldn't drop that bombshell now, not when his every move seemed to infuriate her.

'It means you clearly enjoy being single.' She smiled brightly. 'I know the type.'

Conrad sighed. They'd clearly got off to a terrible start and, by the sounds of it, she didn't think much of men.

'Anyway,' she went on, 'I need some sleep. I'll leave you to it.' She backed towards the door, practically vibrating with nervous energy, so all he could do was watch her, bewildered. 'It was... good to meet you.'

'You too.' He replaced the candlestick on the

mantelpiece and followed her from the bedroom into the kitchen, where she made for the front door as if the building were on fire.

'And merry Christmas, for yesterday,' he said as she yanked open the door, letting in a blast of frigid air that made him shiver.

'Merry Christmas,' she said, on a nervous squawk before she kept her stare lowered and fled up the path to her part of the house, leaving Conrad to scratch his head and wonder if he and his wildly sexy English landlady could be any more different.

CHAPTER TWO

A WEEK LATER, on his third shift as a locum obstetrics registrar, Conrad strode onto the labour
ward at Derby's Abbey Hill Hospital, his footsteps slowing to a halt. Up ahead at the nurses'
station stood his incredibly sexy but uptight landlady, Zara Wood. Internally, he groaned, his
heart sinking. To say they'd got off to a bad start
last week was an understatement. He'd never met
anyone as wary as her, and she clearly thought
him some sort of philandering creep. Sadly, that
hadn't stopped him wondering about her inces-
santly, knowing this day, when their paths would
cross again, would come. But if they *had* to work
together, it made sense to clear the air.

Expecting their reunion to be as frosty as the
English winter weather outside, Conrad hesitantly approached, watching Zara, who wore a
harassed expression as she stabbed at the computer keyboard in frustration.

'Do we actually have a registrar working
today?' she asked her midwife colleagues, Sha-

ron and Bella, whom Conrad had already met. 'They don't seem to be answering their pager.'

'We certainly do,' Sharon said with a knowing smile as she wiped patient names off the whiteboard behind the desk. 'Haven't you met our locum?' She winked suggestively at Bella, who chuckled and rolled her eyes.

'Oh…are you in for a treat,' Sharon continued, with her back to Zara. 'In fact, I think he's single. I know I sound like a broken record here, and I know that you "don't need a man"…'

Clearly Zara often threw around this argument.

'But for him,' Sharon said, 'it might be worth finally breaking your long dry spell.'

Conrad hid a smile, his ego posturing as Bella fanned her face dramatically. 'Right…that accent,' she said to Sharon, 'the body, those eyes. I certainly wouldn't kick him out of bed for not emptying the bins. Makes you wanna move to Australia.'

Conrad crept closer on softened footfalls so he could eavesdrop for a little longer. He worked hard at keeping in shape. It was good to know that his efforts at the gym hadn't gone unnoticed. He was only in town for another three weeks, and, after past events in his personal life he was trying not to think about, it had been a long time since he'd felt in a relationship kind of place.

That didn't stop him wondering what Zara Wood really thought about him though.

'Wait,' Zara said, rounding on her colleagues, her back to Conrad and her hands on her hips so he had an uninterrupted view of the gorgeous outline of her figure. 'Did you say Australian?'

Bella nodded and Conrad froze, wondering if Zara would make the connection.

'He's not tall with grey eyes, is he?' she went on. 'A smile that could melt off your clothes?'

His lips twitched as he forced his stare from the curve of Zara's hips, although she'd certainly checked out his nakedness a week ago, before she'd torn a few strips off him and almost kicked him out of the flat he'd legally rented. But it was good to hear confirmation that their attraction, their chemistry, was mutual.

'Yes, that's the one,' Sharon said as she wrote new names on the board. 'Dr Reed.'

'Oh, no…' Zara muttered, her shoulders sagging.

'So you *have* met?' Sharon turned to fully face Zara, a delighted smile on her face. Then the older woman caught sight of Conrad in the background, her eyes widening with surprise and a flicker of guilt.

'Good afternoon, ladies,' he said, announcing himself with a straight face. 'Did I hear my name mentioned?' He came to a halt behind Zara, who seemed to freeze, her shoulders tensing.

Zara spun on her heel, her expression impressively innocent considering how they'd just been gossiping about him. 'Of course you're a doctor here…' she muttered stonily. 'I suspected as much when I saw your stethoscope hanging by the door last week.' Her voice was clipped with annoyance and accusation, telling him he was in trouble again. But at least she wasn't wielding a weapon this time.

'That's right. A locum.' Conrad smiled and dropped his voice, unable to resist teasing her again. 'But at least this week I've got my clothes on.'

Despite trying very hard to look busy, the other two midwives were obviously shamelessly eavesdropping, because they gaped excitedly and then hid stunned smiles.

'You couldn't have mentioned that you worked at *my* hospital when we met?' Zara said, ignoring the delighted, slightly impressed mirth of her colleagues. She grabbed one of the ward tablets from the charging station and glared his way, clearly still furious with him.

'I had planned on bringing it up when I saw your name badge,' he said, his lips twitching as he glanced down from her green-brown eyes to where she clutched the device the way she'd gripped that candlestick—with malicious intent. 'But my fight-or-flight response got in the way. You looked menacing wielding that candlestick.'

Zara sighed and glanced at her colleagues, who were pretending not to listen. 'It's not what it seems.'

Sharon and Bella looked up, innocently.

'She's right,' he added. 'It was just a simple misunderstanding.'

'Okay, okay, don't protest too much. We believe you,' Sharon said, eyeing Zara with an impressed and questioning look. Clearly Sharon *didn't* believe them and wanted all the juicy details. In trying to smooth over their misunderstanding, he'd only made it worse.

'I thought he was a squatter,' Zara exclaimed to the other women, 'so I accidentally confronted him getting out of the shower. He's renting my basement flat, although he's one infringement shy of being evicted.'

Zara returned her glare to Conrad and the other two midwives chuckled and trailed away, back to work.

'As we're housemates as well as colleagues...' Conrad said with his most charming smile. How had she described it? Capable of melting off clothes? He could work with that. 'I take it you won't mind me calling you Zara?'

Her eyes narrowed with suspicion. 'As you're

finally here,' she said, pointedly, 'I have a thirty-three-year-old primip who's been in second-stage labour for forty-five minutes that I'd like you to examine.' Without further preamble, she marched down the ward, heading for one of the delivery rooms as if he were an obedient dog who would come to heel.

Conrad followed, setting aside the invigorating friction with his prickly landlady for now, although it was certainly helping him to forget why he'd as good as run away from Australia to hide for a while in deepest, darkest midwinter England.

He paused outside the delivery room to wash his hands. 'I take it the foetal heart rate is stable? No sign of distress?' he asked, his mind now on work.

'It is, but mum-to-be is pretty exhausted. She's been labouring for eighteen hours.' She pressed her lips together as if Conrad were to blame for her patient's predicament.

'Have the membranes ruptured?' he asked, tossing the paper towels in the bin.

'Yes, and the neonatal registrar is on their way,' Zara replied, pushing open the door and nodding to the other midwife in the room before addressing the patient.

'Angela, this is Dr Reed, the obstetrician. I've asked him to examine you because you've been pushing for a while now and this baby doesn't seem to want to be born.'

As another contraction took hold of their patient, Conrad observed the foetal heart monitor for signs of distress and pulled on some sterile gloves.

'Angela,' he said, 'on the next contraction, I just need to examine you, okay?'

The woman nodded, bracing herself as another wave of pain struck. Conrad quickly examined the birth canal, felt the baby's head and the fully dilated cervix before meeting Zara's stare. 'The baby is right occiput-transverse,' Conrad told her.

Zara nodded, a flash of relief in her big expressive eyes.

'The baby is absolutely fine,' Conrad explained to Angela and her partner, a concerned-looking guy with round glasses and dark curly hair. 'But its head is a little rotated. He or she needs a little bit of help coming out, so, if you agree, I'm going to use the ventouse suction to help things along.'

Angela nodded weakly, her grip tightening on her partner's hand as another contraction took hold. Zara set up the instrument tray for the delivery while the second midwife assisted Angela through her contractions and her breathing. The neonatal registrar arrived, the small delivery room filling up with bodies. While the baby seemed fine at the moment, instrumental delivery could be a traumatic experience and the newborn would need checking immediately after birth.

'Okay,' Conrad said to all concerned. 'Let's get this little one delivered.' He slipped on fresh gloves and set up the instrument, while Zara positioned herself at his side, the second midwife and the partner holding the patient's hands.

'On the next contraction, Angela,' Zara instructed, 'Dr Reed is going to straighten the baby's head and apply suction, okay? You keep pushing until we tell you to stop and soon you'll have your baby.'

With that familiar surge of adrenaline in his veins, Conrad attached the suction cup to the top of the baby's head and applied gentle traction while rotating slightly to reposition the baby's head. He never tired of the thrill of helping to welcome a human being into the world. He loved his job, and it was immediately obvious that so too did Zara. At least that was one thing they had in common.

With the baby's head in the usual position of occiput-anterior, the next contraction delivered the baby's head.

'Okay, Angela, pant now,' Zara instructed, watching his every move.

Conrad quickly removed the cord from around the baby's neck, becoming aware that Zara was tightly gripping his shoulder, as if fully invested in the safe delivery of her patient's baby.

In the pause between contractions, Conrad glanced up and met her stare, a flicker of respect blooming in his chest. Given they'd be living together and working together for a few weeks, it made sense that they try and get along. Life was too short for disagreements and misunderstandings.

'Just one more push now,' Zara told the mother, releasing Conrad's shoulder with a slightly embarrassed shrug, 'and you'll meet your baby.'

Now that the hardest part of the delivery was over, Conrad shifted sideways to make room for the feisty but fascinating midwife. As an obstetric trainee, he'd soon learned how midwives could be very possessive of the babies they delivered. Where midwifery specialised in normal pregnancy and birth, Conrad was only really required when things weren't going to plan. That said, the specialities depended on one another. Everyone involved in obstetrics was there for the same reason: to ensure the safety of both the mother and the baby.

The baby's shoulders were delivered with the next contraction, followed by the rest of the newborn, a baby boy with a lusty cry and a full head of dark hair just like his father. Conrad detached the suction cup from the baby's head and wheeled his stool aside to allow Zara close enough to lift the newborn onto his mother's stomach.

'You have a son,' Zara said. 'Congratulations.' Her eyes shone with emotion as she supervised Dad to cut the umbilical cord.

Conrad smiled to himself, glad that the situation was so easily resolved. While the tearful couple met their baby, Conrad assessed the woman's birth canal for damage. 'Just the placenta to deliver now, Angela, then I just need to give you a couple of stitches and we're all done.'

The woman nodded her consent, too in awe of the new life in her arms to worry about the business end of things, so Conrad got to work. The room emptied of the now redundant extra bodies—the neonatal registrar and the second midwife—leaving Conrad and Zara alone with the new family.

'I'll bring you some toast and tea,' Zara said to Angela as Conrad finished up the sutures and pulled a blanket over Angela's legs.

'Congratulations,' he said, taking a second to glance at the contented newborn, who, after all the excitement, had dozed off to sleep, before leaving the new family to get to know each other.

He found Zara in the ward kitchen, making toast.

'I feel like we got off to a bad start last week,' he said, slouching against the door frame and

watching her brusque movements with fascina-
tion. 'We should probably try to get along, seeing that we're not only working together but also
living in the same house, don't you think?'

She shot him a sideways glance. He raised his
eyebrows expectantly, his pulse bounding with
excitement, because he'd been right earlier: their
attraction was clearly mutual.

'Did you have to mention the lack of clothes
in front of my colleagues earlier?' she said, eyes
narrowed with suspicion. 'It sounded bad.'

'I'm sorry. I didn't mean for them to hear.
And I was just teasing you. I hoped to coax out
a smile after the misunderstanding of our first
meeting.'

'It seems everything's a joke to you,' she
huffed. 'But you should know that it's hard to
keep a secret around here.'

'That's a bit harsh,' he said, wondering exactly
how he'd managed to get so far under her skin. 'I
take my work very seriously. And I did overhear
you all talking about me behind my back earlier.
Why don't we call it even and call a truce?'

His apology, the reminder that he'd been the
topic of some pretty unprofessional conversation,
seemed to appease some of her indignation, but
not all of it, because she went on. 'I know you
seemed to have charmed everyone else here with

your... This...' She waved her finger in his general direction.

'With my *clothes-melting smile*?' he offered, enjoying the sparks in her stare. But he rarely clicked with someone this strongly and instantly.

Her scowl deepened. 'But, just for the record, you're wasting your time trying to charm me. I work and take care of my son. That's all I have time for.'

'Noted,' he said, his expression serious. 'It can't be easy being a single parent. I take my hat off to you.'

Ignoring his comment, she looked up sharply. 'So you understand that I'm not interested in being your next casual conquest?' She shot him a pitying smirk, even though *she* was the one rumoured to be stuck in a prolonged dry spell. But his first impressions had clearly been spot on. Zara Wood obviously had no time for men. And despite finding his landlady incredibly attractive, Conrad hadn't dated seriously for over six years.

'Of course I do. But from what I've seen of Morholme,' he added about the village just outside Derby where they both lived, 'we seem to be the only two residents under the age of sixty. I'm only in the UK for another three weeks, but it makes sense for you and I to at least be friendly, don't you think? After all, life is too short for drama.'

Sadly, he knew that first hand. His brother's violent death six months earlier had been sudden and shocking. A man he'd loved and looked up to, there one minute and inexplicably gone the next when all he'd been doing was his job. It had made Conrad all too aware of the fleeting nature of life. You could lose what you loved in a split second.

Conrad dragged his thoughts from his still fresh grief and watched Zara set her features in an unreadable expression. 'I don't have much time for friends, so don't get your hopes up.' She smirked. 'You might want to consider other forms of…entertainment.'

Of course, by entertainment she meant sex. Because she'd obviously picked up on his casual attitude to dating, something he'd perfected over the past six years, since he'd moved too fast and been dumped.

'I understand,' he said with a smile, desperately trying to work his charm. 'But I was really just talking about a friendly coffee between two colleagues.' It was her mind that had turned immediately to sex. 'I don't want any awkwardness between us; that's not my style. Do you have a break coming up?' he asked, gratified to see her flush.

If they didn't have to work together *and* live together, he'd have given up trying to win her over by now. But there was something about her he couldn't seem to ignore. Despite their misunderstanding and their other differences, she, like him, was a straight talker. After the betrayals of his past from the one person he'd trusted more than anyone else, his late brother, he instantly respected that about Zara.

'I'm due a break in ten minutes,' she said, placing the buttered toast on a tray with two mugs of strong tea. 'I'll finish up with Angela and meet you in the staff canteen.'

'Great,' he said, his heart banging as if he'd won an epic victory. 'Coffee is on me.'

She raised her chin. 'I can buy my own coffee, thanks.'

Feisty and fiercely independent… 'Got it.' He sighed. What was it about Zara Wood that intrigued him?

'I'll see you later.' With an inscrutable glance, she picked up the tray and passed him, the sway of her hips as she walked down the ward his only reward for bravely extending the Anglo-Australian olive branch.

CHAPTER THREE

TEN MINUTES LATER, in the cafeteria, a flustered Zara took the seat opposite Conrad. What were the chances that her Australian lodger was also the new obstetric locum? If only she'd asked him what he did for a living that first day instead of shamelessly ogling him and judging him for being young, free and single, she might have avoided further embarrassment.

'Thanks for coming,' he said, all easy charm, those grey eyes of his smiling.

Zara shrugged, still mortified that he'd overheard her comments on his attractiveness earlier. But at least he hadn't gloated too much. She unwrapped her sandwich, although her stomach clenched with nerves. She blamed her colleagues on the delivery ward. The minute Sharon and Bella had discovered she was meeting the new locum doctor, who also happened to be her tenant, for a coffee, they'd shrieked like a couple of silly excited schoolgirls. Matchmaker Sharon, who was always encouraging Zara to *live a little* and *have fun*, had even fussed with Zara's hair and tried to persuade her to put on some lip gloss. As if...

'So, what brings you all the way to the middle of England from Australia?' she asked, trying her best to be friendly. 'As you pointed out, it's not for our barbecue weather,' she scoffed.

Outside, it was another dreary, grey and bitterly cold winter's day. But no matter what the state of the weather, she couldn't seem to forget she'd seen him stark naked. That was what six years without sex did to you.

'I finished my registrar training back in Australia, but I didn't want to apply for a consultant post yet.' Conrad smiled that killer smile, shrugging casually as if his easy-going personality was natural and in no way contrived. 'So I applied for a locum position and here I am.'

He took a sip of his coffee and she forced herself to take a bite of the sandwich, knowing from past experience she should take the opportunity to eat while she could. But despite all her tough talk, despite blaming Sharon for her nerves, there was something about Dr Reed that made her edgy.

Maybe because they were opposites, chalk and cheese. Maybe because he was the first Australian she'd ever met. Maybe because he was the only man in six years she'd found attractive enough to make her wonder if Sharon was right when it came to dating and sex and relationships: Zara *was* selling herself short. And she had to reluctantly admit that, whatever his other faults, he seemed to be good at his job.

But she didn't suffer fools. She'd meant what she'd said. His charisma, the good looks, the hot body—all irrelevant. She'd fallen for that kind of charm offensive once before. Zach's father had been one of *those* guys—avoiding commitment or being tied down, simply out for a good time. Her mistake had come with consequences for the most precious person in her life: her son.

'I actually like the contrast,' he said, still referring to the weather. 'Where I'm from, winter temperatures rarely drop below twelve degrees Celsius.'

Zara sneered, wondering again why he'd come all the way to the middle of England in the winter. She couldn't imagine that Derby, or even Morholme, would be anyone's choice of travel destination. Looking at his light tan, the sun-kissed ends of his hair, the laughter lines around his eyes and mouth, Zara imagined the exotic heat and golden sand beaches of Australia, a place of surfing and picnics and laid-back vibes. A place she'd never been.

'Where in Australia are you from?' she asked, thawing to him a little, not that she wanted him to know she'd spent the past week daydreaming about her sexy new tenant or furtively hoping for another glimpse of him leaving the flat. When Bella had mentioned the new doctor was Australian, she'd even secretly hoped him and her lodger, the only Australian she knew, were one and the same.

'Brisbane,' he said, watching her intently as if, to him, she was equally exotic. 'Well, the Sunshine Coast to be precise.'

Zara rolled her eyes disbelievingly. *The Sunshine Coast...?* That sounds like a dreadful place to live. No wonder you prefer sleepy, freezing-cold Morholme.' What on earth was he doing there?

He laughed, his smile lighting those gorgeous grey eyes that seemed to bore into hers. Zara couldn't help but smile back. It had been a long time since she'd clicked with a man or found a shared sense of humour, not that this mild flirtation could go anywhere, of course.

'Have you ever been to Australia?' he asked, something in his laid-back attitude surprisingly intriguing now that she knew he took his work seriously, something she could respect.

Zara shook her head. 'No. I've always wanted to visit. It's on my list.' She didn't want to tell him the last time she'd been abroad she'd been a twenty-year-old student midwife. She'd saved up for a friends' holiday to Spain, where she'd fallen for a handsome Spanish waiter, had a dreamy holiday romance and come home pregnant. She already felt pretty unworldly compared to Conrad Reed.

And the last thing she wanted to think about in front of him was her youthful naivety and how, even after all these years, there was a part of her that blamed herself for Zach's situation. Holiday romances never lasted, and she didn't regret having her wonderful boy. But she wished she'd chosen a better father for him, one interested in knowing him, even if he and Zara weren't together.

'Holidays for me are usually a rainy week in South Wales.' She shrugged, her face heating. 'Or a road trip to Chester Zoo, but I wouldn't change a thing, obviously.'

She pressed her lips together, experiencing the familiar sharp ache of rejection on Zach's behalf. Spain wasn't that far away from England, and if Lorenzo had asked, she'd have brought baby Zach to meet his father. Instead she'd learned just how little she'd meant to the Spanish waiter, who probably had a different fling with a fresh holidaymaker every two weeks. A man like that, just selfishly out for a good time, had no use for a kid cramping his style.

'So, how old is your son?' Conrad asked, seeming genuinely interested.

'Zach. He's five.'

Conrad raised his eyebrows, his smile filled with satisfaction. 'Same age as my nephew, James.' Something shifted over his expression—pride, longing, a flicker of sadness, gone before she could be sure of it. 'Is he at school?'

Zara nodded, instinctively sensing that Conrad and James were close. She recognised the adoring look on his face. 'He goes to Morholme Primary School.'

'So how do you juggle shift work and childcare?'

'I'm lucky to have my mum living close by. She often picks Zach up from school while I'm at work. And, depending on my pattern of shifts, has him for sleepovers, which he loves.' In many ways, she had a great life: a good job she adored, a secure home thanks to her father, a son who made her smile, every day. No wonder she couldn't find the energy to bother with something as dissatisfying as dating, not when, in her experience, men were so unreliable.

'So is your nephew in Australia?' she asked, curious that they seemed to have the love of a five-year-old in common. Would she need to revise her first impressions of this man?

'Yeah, in Brisbane. I miss the little guy.' He

glanced down at his coffee, telling her he didn't want to say more on the subject.

'It must be quite a culture shock for you coming here,' she said. 'Derby isn't exactly a cosmopolitan city and there's literally nothing to do in Morholme unless you're into pensioners' bingo at the village hall.'

He laughed again, meeting her stare. 'Morholme is very quaint, I guess. But you've done a beautiful job with the flat. It's very comfortable.' His expression was full of warmth and curiosity that left Zara aware of his observation to the tips of her fingers and toes.

'Thank you,' she said, his compliment bringing an unexpected ache to her throat. 'My father left me the house, so Zach and I are lucky.'

'Your father has passed?' he asked, with a frown.

'Yes, five years ago, just after Zach was born. He had pancreatic cancer.' Why was she telling him this? She barely knew him. But he was right; life *was* short. Her father's untimely death was proof of that. Not a day went by where she didn't miss her dad. She owed her parents so much. She could never have finished her midwifery training and established herself at the hospital without the support from Pam and, thanks to her father, she and Zach would always have a roof over their heads.

'I'm sorry,' he said, simply. 'I understand what that's like. I've lost someone, too.'

Zara blinked away the sting in her eyes. 'Then I'm sorry, too,' she said, feeling awkward and wondering if the real reason he'd left Australia was to mourn.

'So what *do* you do for fun, *Ms* Wood,' he asked, pasting on a bright smile and changing the subject, 'if it's not pensioners' bingo at the village hall?'

Zara smiled, grateful that they could shift back to lighter topics. 'Well, nothing as exciting as I'm imagining you do on the Sunshine Coast, perhaps barbecues and beach walks.' If only he knew how mundane her life was—not that she needed his pity. She and Zach were fine.

She smiled a genuine smile, thinking about her son. 'After a week of juggling childcare and shift work, the highlight of my week is usually feeding the ducks at the village pond on a Sunday, followed by a trip to the playground.' There was nothing better than spending time with her little boy, the centre of her world. If her own personal life lacked a certain…sizzle, it was a small price to pay for Zach's happiness and security.

'So no New Year's Eve party lined up for tonight?' he asked. 'Perhaps a hot date?' His stare glittered with that curiosity that told her their attraction was obviously mutual, even if they had no intention of acting on it. 'I heard mention of a dry spell earlier, so I just wondered…'

Zara blushed furiously. She couldn't even recall what a *hot date* felt like. In fact, she'd barely had a couple before having Zach. But she was going to throttle Sharon. 'No, no date tonight.' And she'd already declined an invite to drinks at Sharon's house.

'Really?' he asked with flattering astonishment. 'But New Year's Eve only comes around once a year. You're too young and too interesting *not* to have a date tonight.'

Zara shrugged, abandoning the rest of her sandwich, because her appetite had vanished. While his comments were flattering, she felt the need to defend herself. 'I'll probably have an early night, actually, given I have the early shift tomorrow and Zach spends every Friday sleeping over at his grandma's. She has a little dog he adores, and she spoils him. But I don't mind.'

He nodded, and she continued her justifications. 'Besides, I've kind of had my fingers burned in the past. I've raised Zach single-handed. My spare time is precious. I'd rather give it all to my son.' And having made one mistake with her holiday romance, having exposed her innocent baby boy to his father's rejection, she just couldn't face the effort of meeting some stranger who'd most likely do a runner as soon as she mentioned she was a single mum.

'Of course,' he said with a guilty wince. 'It must be a lot to juggle.'

'What about you?' she asked, desperate to change the subject back to Conrad. 'Any kids of your own? A wife or girlfriend back in Australia? Or maybe both?'

She needed some nugget of information she could give to Sharon and Bella when she returned to the ward. Her colleagues would be hungry to know what she and the hunky Australian had talked about, and Sharon would go ballistic if all Zara had done was talk about why she was so sworn off relationships.

He shrugged, looking mildly uncomfortable for the first time. 'I've dated in the past, but, you know, nothing serious in recent years.'

She sensed there might be more to the story, but, like her, he obviously didn't want to talk about his past relationships. 'You're just having a good time, right?'

Why was she poking at him this way? She wasn't normally rude. But there was something about him that was forcing her to revise her first impressions and messing with her head. She blamed Sharon, who'd acted as if Zara were going on a real date, when in reality *she* wouldn't know a good time if it came up and kissed her senseless.

'You don't think much of me, do you, Zara?' He smiled, holding her eye contact for a long while, making her squirm.

'I don't know you,' she said, all bluster now that he'd called her out. 'But I think you're a good doctor. You paid your rent on time. The rest is none of my business.'

He laughed and Zara couldn't help but smile too, glad to pretend she'd been joking, because, otherwise, she'd sounded like a bitter old shrew who judged every man she met against her disappointment with Zach's father.

But now that she'd met this sexy Australian with such a different outlook from hers, the huge hole in her personal life gaped open. If she didn't know better, she'd think he'd been sent there to shake up the life she'd assumed she had under control and make her restless for something more. She'd just cast that ridiculous thought out of her head when Conrad's pager sounded an urgent tone.

'It's Labour Ward,' he said, looking down, abandoning what was left of his coffee and jerking to his feet.

'I'll come with you.' Even though she had fifteen minutes of her break left, Zara grabbed her bag and they both started running.

The alarm led them to one of the delivery rooms. Sharon glanced up as they entered, her expression sagging with relief, but Zara's blood froze. She and Sharon had been looking after this woman together, before Zara had gone on her break.

'This is Jane Phillips,' Zara told Conrad. 'A twenty-eight-year-old multiparous mum on her third pregnancy.'

More help arrived: the obstetrics SHO, Max, and a crash team anaesthetist.

'Normal vaginal delivery four minutes ago,' Sharon added in a panicked voice, her stare flicking to the newborn in the arms of the father, who was looking on anxiously. 'Sudden post-partum haemorrhage following third stage,' Sharon continued, reaching to the wall behind the new mother to adjust the flow of oxygen to a mask she fitted over Jane's face.

Conrad grabbed a wide bore cannula and a tourniquet, quickly introducing himself to the patient as he sited the cannula in her arm.

'We need cross match. Four units,' he said, extracting a blood sample and passing it to Max.

While Sharon set up an infusion of intravenous fluids, and Zara drew up syntocinon, a drug that would contract the uterus and hopefully slow down the bleeding, Conrad placed a hand on Jane's abdomen, manually massaging the uterus.

'Start the syntocinon transfusion,' Conrad told Zara, his alarm obvious in the clipped tone of his voice. 'Was the placenta intact?' he asked Sharon.

'I thought so.' Sharon nodded as the woman's blood pressure dropped, the alarms sounding once more.

With panic and fear in charge of her heart rate, Zara took over the compression of the uterus while Conrad examined the patient.

'There's no obvious tear,' he said, meeting Zara's stare. 'The bleeding is coming from high up. Keep massaging.' He reached for a second intravenous cannula and sited it in the woman's other arm, the sense of urgency in the room building. Catastrophic post-partum haemorrhage was fortunately rare but life-threatening, and every midwife and obstetrician's worst nightmare.

'If we can't get the bleeding to stop,' Zara explained to the alarmed couple, who hadn't had a chance to enjoy their newborn baby, 'you might need to go to Theatre.'

'Get a second bag of fluids up, please,' Conrad told Sharon, who rushed to do his bidding. 'Zara, can you draw up some prostaglandin?' asked Conrad as they nervously watched the blood pressure monitor, willing the drugs to work and the bleeding to slow.

Zara reached for the second line drug as Conrad took over with the uterine massage, their efforts coordinated, their differences and misunderstandings forgotten as they worked as a team.

Zara injected the prostaglandin into the muscle of Jane's thigh and looked to Conrad for guidance.

'Blood loss isn't slowing as quickly as I would like,' he said, addressing the patient and her partner. 'Do you consent to surgery?'

The couple nodded, wide-eyed now with the same fear Zara was desperately trying to control.

'Call Theatre,' Conrad told Sharon, clearly reaching the limit of his composure. 'Tell them we're on our way.' He unlocked the wheels of the bed and nodded to Zara. 'Take over here with uterine compression and, Max, get the blood sent round to Theatre.'

Leaving Dad and the baby in Sharon's care, she, Conrad and the anaesthetist steered the patient out of the delivery room and rushed towards the lifts that would take them straight to the operating suites.

Inside the department, Zara handed the patient over to the waiting theatre staff, her job for now done. 'Keep me posted,' she told Conrad as the doors swung closed.

He gave her a determined nod. Of respect, of thanks, of promise. Then he disappeared out of sight, racing to surgery with their patient. Zara headed back to the delivery ward, her adrenaline draining away to be replaced by concern. She hoped for their patient's sake, for Jane's newborn and her husband, that her instincts were right: that Conrad *was* a good surgeon. For now, all she could do was wait.

CHAPTER FOUR

LATER THAT NIGHT, back in Morholme, Conrad knocked on Zara's front door, nervous excitement making his heart skip a beat. He understood how Zara's alternating shifts created issues with childcare, but he hated the idea of her being alone on New Year's Eve. He waited in the freezing pitch black. Days were dark when he arrived at work in the morning and dark again by the time he left the hospital in the evening. It made him wonder if he'd ever again see the sun.

The door opened and Zara appeared, her expression one of surprise. Warmth flooded onto the doorstep from the house. She looked relaxed and sexy in her jeans and sweater. She'd been on his mind all day since their talk in the cafeteria and the emergency they'd dealt with together.

'Hi,' he said, trying to keep his voice serious. 'I wondered if you could point me in the direction of pensioners' bingo? I hear it's the most exciting thing that happens around here.'

Her laughter lit her eyes and raised his sun-starved spirits, so his smile widened. There was something about her laugh, her sense of humour, that mocking challenge in her stare, that took his mind off his own troubles. She'd admitted she'd had her fingers burned when it came to dating, and he wondered how far her trust issues went. That would be another thing they had in common, although Conrad's own sense of betrayal was complex and snared up with his grief over losing his brother, Marcus. It was hard to be angry with a dead man, especially one Conrad had always looked up to, the one person he'd thought he could trust.

'Actually,' he went on, keen to change the direction of his thoughts away from his late brother, and his reasons for leaving Australia so he'd had space to think and grieve, 'I'm going to try out the local pub, and wondered if you'd like to join me, seeing as you're alone tonight and we're probably the only two non-retired people in the whole of Morholme.'

A moment's hesitation flicked over her expression. 'Um… I have to be up at five.'

'I know, but it's New Year's Eve. We don't have to stay long, but I hear there's live music,' he cajoled playfully, switching on the smile she found charming, 'a buffet, and, if you need further convincing, even a meat raffle donated by the local butcher! How could you possibly resist?'

She laughed again, her refusal clearly waning.

'We might have a good time,' he urged. 'I don't know about you, but after today, I could use a few laughs.'

At mention of their emergency, she seemed to change her mind, to his relief. 'Sure, why not? Although I can't promise I'll make it to midnight. And I hope you like your beer warm and your sandwiches curly, not a barbecued prawn in sight.'

'They're my favourite, as it happens,' he joked, elated that he'd managed to persuade her and draw her a little more out of her shell. Today, he'd revised his opinion that she was prickly and up-tight. She was smart and funny. She was clearly a dedicated midwife and was understandably de-voted to her young son. When she let down her guard, her attractiveness shot through the roof. When she laughed with him, he didn't miss Aus-tralia quite as much.

'I'll just grab my coat.' She disappeared for a second, reappearing wearing boots, a puffer jacket and woollen hat with a furry pompom. They set off on the short walk to the Miner's Arms, side by side.

'So how did the surgery go?' she asked.

'Thanks for texting me to say she was out of Theatre, by the way.'

'You're welcome. I'm not going to lie, it was stressful,' he said, watching a small frown of worry tug at her mouth. 'I found some retained placental tissue that was causing the bleeding, so she lost a lot of blood.' Post-partum haemorrhage was one of the worst emergencies he ever had to treat.

Zara glanced up at him with obvious concern. 'You were still in Theatre when my shift ended, so I've been worrying about the outcome. Will she be okay?'

Conrad nodded. 'I hope so. I had to transfuse three litres of blood and her renal function went off a bit. So she's recovering on the high-dependency unit for now, but I hope to transfer her to the postnatal ward in the morning, as long as she's remained stable overnight. How was the baby?' he asked, recalling how emotional and exhausted the husband had been when Conrad had spoken to him on HDU.

Zara's frown eased slightly. 'He's well. Perfectly healthy. So that's one good thing.'

'Yeah.' He dragged in a deep breath. 'Sometimes it's hard to leave the job behind, isn't it?' There was something very attractive about Zara's dedication to her patients. It spoke of loyalty and compassion, two very attractive qualities in Conrad's book.

'It is,' she agreed. 'It can be emotionally draining.'

'That's why I'm so glad I could persuade you to come for a drink tonight.'

She smiled and some of the tension around her eyes eased. 'Why did you choose obstetrics?' she asked, eyeing him with curiosity as they crossed the deserted road towards the quintessential English pub, which had brass carriage lamps beside the door and climbing ivy growing along the stonework.

'Well, my mother is a midwife,' he said, pulling open the door to the pub for Zara to enter first, 'and, believe it or not, I like the happy endings. If we do our jobs right, we not only help the patient, but we also send her home a mother to a healthy baby. That's pretty cool in my book.'

'I agree, it is,' Zara said, her observation intensifying as if she'd warmed to him since their earlier chat in the hospital canteen. And the feeling was mutual. Faced with an evening alone with only his ruminations on why he was there in England, Conrad had remembered Zara say her son was spending the night at her mum's place. The idea of getting to know her a bit better, a woman who'd pretty much been on his mind since the day they met, had galvanised him off the sofa.

Inside the Miner's Arms, the antiquated theme continued with low ceilings criss-crossed with wooden beams, old guys in flat caps propping up the bar and a roaring log fire in a massive blackened grate.

'What can I get you,' he asked over the sound of the band, who were playing popular classics no one was dancing to.

Zara removed her hat and unzipped her coat, her cheeks rosy from the cold. 'I'll have a pint of Chatsworth Gold ale, please.'

Conrad nodded, impressed by her drink of choice. While Zara smiled at a few locals and wandered off to find them a table near the fire, he ordered two pints of Chatsworth Gold, his attraction to his landlady building. He wasn't looking for a relationship. He was only in the UK for another three weeks. But Zara Wood was exactly his type: stunning, smart, funny and clearly dedicated to her work and her son.

Wondering again about her dry spell and what it meant for a harmless bit of flirtation, he joined her at the table and took a seat.

'Cheers,' he said, raising his glass. 'To the end of a busy week and the end of another year.'

'Cheers!' She smiled and clinked her glass to his, taking a sip.

'Oh, that's good,' he said, the hops and honey blending on his tongue.

'As good as your Australian beer?' she asked, her hazel eyes twinkling in the glow from the fire.

'Better,' he said. 'And perfectly chilled too. You promised me warm beer...'

'Well, warm beer is the house special,' she teased. 'You have to ask for it with a secret hand-shake.' She winked. 'I'll teach it to you.'

Conrad laughed, delighted that she seemed to be enjoying herself. 'Obviously beer drinking is how you Brits manage your seasonal mood disorders,' he countered. 'Is winter always this dark? I literally haven't seen the sun for days.'

'Don't be such a baby,' she said, laughing at him.

Conrad basked in the sound, his curiosity for this woman building to an unreachable itch. 'What made you change your mind about joining me tonight?'

'It's a woman's prerogative,' she said. Then she shrugged, mischief in her eyes. 'Actually, I think it was your willingness to eat curly sandwiches, or maybe what you said earlier about life being short and New Year's Eve only coming around once a year. As you might have overheard this morning, Sharon is always trying to fix me up with single men, although dating is the last thing on my mind. Don't tell her about this, by the way. She's a dreadful matchmaker. If she finds out we had an innocent drink, she'll have us married by next Tuesday.'

'Your secret is safe with me.' He smiled, something she'd said earlier niggling at him. 'So, is Zach's father in the picture at all?'

At his mention of her son's name, she looked surprised, as if she hadn't expected him to listen or to remember.

'Nope,' she said, with a shake of her head. 'It was a holiday fling. He's Spanish. When he found out he was going to be a father, he declined the offer to stay in touch.' She shrugged, her eyes darting away as if she was embarrassed. 'And can you really be called a father if by choice you've never met your son or contributed to his life in any way?'

'I guess not.' He winced, appalled on Zara and Zach's behalf. 'So he doesn't even support Zach financially?'

She shook her head again, looking uncomfortable. 'But I see to it that Zach has everything he needs.'

Conrad nodded, the steely glint in her eyes highlighting the fierce independence he both admired and wondered if it masked more vulnerable feelings. 'I'm sorry,' he said. 'That's his loss.'

She glanced at him sharply, as if he'd caught

her off guard in return. 'It's fine. My son doesn't need a male role model like that.'

'So is he the reason you don't date, even if you had time?' he asked, cautiously, wary of crossing the line and upsetting her again. He hated that someone with so much going for her had closed off that part of her life. She was in her mid-twenties, way too young to have sworn off relationships, although these days, he too took things slow.

Zara flushed, shifting in her seat. 'Don't get me wrong, I like men, well, the dependable, responsible ones, that is.' She shrugged. 'I guess I've had to learn to rely on myself and it's become a bit of a habit. And I go out of my way to ensure my mistake doesn't define my son or allow him to suffer in any way.'

'Fair enough.' He nodded because he'd made his own mistakes, rushed into a relationship with the last serious girlfriend he'd had, like the proverbial fool, and lost her. Of course, the heartache he'd experienced when she'd broken up with him was nothing compared to the sense of betrayal he'd known later when she'd moved on to his brother. It seemed he hadn't in fact lost her because he'd moved too fast. Tessa just hadn't wanted Conrad.

'So what would New Year's Eve in Brisbane look like?' Zara asked, drawing him away from thoughts he always seemed to get snagged on: how the brother he'd loved and looked up to could have deceived and betrayed him like that.

'Definite beer consumption,' he said, smiling through the flicker of homesickness pinching his ribs. 'Parties in every bar and restaurant along the river. Fireworks at midnight.'

She looked wistful for a second, before she blinked the expression away. 'You must miss home?'

'I miss some things.' Conrad paused, taking another swallow of the delicious ale. 'Family, obviously—my parents, my nephew. The weather...' His smile stretched, and he realised he was already pretty addicted to drawing out Zara Wood's brand of throaty laughter. First impressions aside, they actually shared quite a bit in common.

'Tell me about James,' she said. 'You two are obviously very close.'

'We are.' Conrad swallowed, his chest hollowing out with a sudden rush of sadness. 'Although I haven't seen him for a while, but he loves dinosaurs and anything with wheels, particularly trains.'

'Don't you live close by in Australia?' she pushed, her stare shifting over his face as she tried to figure him out.

'I do,' he admitted, reluctant to spill the complexities of his past, despite feeling relaxed from the beer and the warmth of the fire and already pretty confident that Zara was a loyal person. 'But... Well, the person I lost recently was my brother, James's dad. Six months ago.'

She gasped, her hand coming to rest on his arm and her stare full of that compassion she shared with her patients. 'I'm so sorry; that's terrible.'

He shrugged, still getting used to saying the words aloud. 'Obviously my sister-in-law, Tessa, is still in a pretty bad place. She's grieving, and you know how hard it is to raise a child alone.'

Of course, his relationship with both Marcus and Tessa had already been strained, before Marcus's death. How could it not have been, given that Conrad and Tessa had once dated, way before she'd slept with Marcus and fallen immediately pregnant with James. Not that it was *her* betrayal that stuck in Conrad's throat. His romantic feelings for Tessa had been long gone by the time she'd hooked up with Marcus. But his brother had owed him some consideration and loyalty and an explanation. Instead they'd sneaked around behind Conrad's back.

'But she's not alone,' Zara pointed out. 'She had you and your parents, right?'

'Yeah.' He nodded, glancing away. 'But since the funeral, Tessa has kind of withdrawn from our family out of grief, taking James with her, obviously.'

'I'm so sorry,' she whispered.

Conrad shrugged. 'When James was born, I promised my brother I'd always look out for him. But after he died, I obviously overdid the concern. Tessa told me to back off. So I figured I'd get away for a few weeks so we all had some space to grieve for Marcus.' And, of course, his and Tessa's history had also clouded the issue.

'So you chose a locum position in the UK?'

He nodded. 'I understand that Tessa is dealing with a lot,' he went on, 'but I miss James. I just hope that when I return to Brisbane, she's ready to let us back into his life.'

'I hope so too, for your sake and for your parents.' Her frown deepened and he could have kicked himself for killing the mood. But he was still trying to get used to talking about Marcus's senseless death without his voice breaking, still trying to make sense of it all.

'It's…complicated,' he said. In more ways than one. 'But the last thing we want to do is push Tessa further away.'

'Do you mind me asking what happened, with your brother?' she whispered when he looked up. 'It's fine if you don't want to talk about it.'

'I don't mind talking about Marcus.' Conrad took a gulp of beer, preparing himself, focussed on the uncomplicated time when Marcus had simply been the older brother he'd looked up to. 'He was amazing. There was only a year between us, so, growing up, we were best friends.'

And that had made the breach of trust harder to bare. He didn't blame Tessa and Marcus for falling in love. But he hated that his brother hadn't come to him straight away, that he'd kept it a secret until discovering Tessa was pregnant, until he'd been forced to come clean. Marcus had tried to heal the rift, and Conrad had been forced to swallow down his sense of betrayal and confusion for the sake of family harmony. But his absolute trust in his brother had been broken, the issue for Conrad going unresolved as life moved on.

'Marcus worked as a paramedic,' he continued, blocking out how he'd felt backed into a corner back then, before James was born, as if his feelings didn't matter because there was a baby coming, a wedding to plan, a sister-in-law to welcome into the Reed family. Then Marcus had died. Conrad's grief was compounded by those lingering feelings of betrayal he'd never quite dealt with. He knew he should let the past go, but he was stuck somehow with no hope of a resolution now that Marcus was gone.

'One day, he attended a call—a case of domestic violence.' Conrad gripped his pint glass, his knuckles white. 'The perpetrator had pushed his wife down the stairs and then called the ambulance. Marcus arrived before the police. He could see from the front door that the woman had a head injury, was lying unconscious and needed urgent help, but he probably should have waited for support. The guy was armed with a knife. He was smart enough to know he was going to jail, so he became belligerent, tried to justify what he'd done. Things escalated when Marcus tried to treat the casualty. He stabbed my brother in the neck before the police arrived. Marcus died later in hospital.'

'That's so terrible.' Zara swallowed hard, her eyes shining with tears. 'So senseless. I'm so sorry.'

Conrad nodded, shocked by how much of the story had come pouring out. But Zara really cared about people. She was easy to talk to.

'Sorry,' he said, drawing a line under the conversation. 'I didn't mean to bring down the mood. It's meant to be a party. It's New Year's Eve.'

'It's okay,' Zara said, her eyes full of empathy. 'I shouldn't have been so curious.'

Conrad eyed their near-empty glasses, eager to pack away his complex feelings for which there seemed to be no end, just an infinite loop. 'I'll um…get us another drink.' He pushed back his chair and stood. 'Unless…' He glanced at the band, who were doing a valiant job considering nearly everyone in the pub was ignoring them. 'Are you up for a dance?' He held out his hand, determined to get the party mood back on track.

Zara frowned at his abrupt change of pace. She looked around the pub, self-consciously. 'Dance…? Really?' She hesitated, eyeing his hand with uncertainty.

Admittedly the place was pretty dead, by New Year's Eve standards, but the band were reasonably good, the tunes catchy and recognisable.

'Definitely,' Conrad said, desperate for her laughter over her pity. If only she knew the other half of the story… 'I've let things get too heavy. And who cares what the old farmers think of us?'

'Okay.' Her eyes glowed with excitement as she put her hand in his, the decision made. Conrad pulled her to her feet and led her to the small carpeted area in front of the makeshift stage, glad to move his body after the serious turn the conversation had taken. With his heart pounding, he scooped his arm around her waist, holding her close, spinning her, making her laugh. The sound shifted the heaviness in his chest to a muted throb he could easily ignore.

Within minutes, another couple had joined them dancing and then another. Zara lost that self-consciousness, throwing herself into enjoying the music as if she hadn't danced in a very long time.

'Now it's a New Year's Eve party,' he said, dipping his head close so he caught the scent of her shampoo, felt the heat of her body, heard the exhilarating catch of her breath.

'It's been a while since I've been to one,' she said, blinking up at him with the same excitement he felt at her closeness. Could she feel this chemistry too? Was she, like him, torn between acting on it or pretending it didn't exist? Whatever happened between them, friendship or more, could only be temporary given he was headed back to Australia in three weeks. But they didn't need to trust each other to have a good time.

'Then I'm glad I persuaded you to come,' he said, simply focussing on enjoying the moment, her company, the building atmosphere, the fact that they were young and alive and on the cusp of a brand-new year.

'Me too.' She smiled and he believed her.

CHAPTER FIVE

'THREE...TWO...ONE. Happy new year!' Zara yelled at the top of her voice as Sid, the normally gruff owner of the Miner's Arms, fired a confetti cannon into the air and gold glittered down on the biggest crowd Zara had ever seen in the village pub.

Conrad scooped her into a big bear hug, his smile infectious. 'Happy new year, Zara,' he said, his warm breath tickling her neck, and the yummy scent of him making her head spin faster than the effects of the alcohol and the party vibe combined. 'I hope it's a great one for you and Zach.'

With her throat choked that he'd included her son in his well wishes and before she could overthink the foreign impulse, she hugged him back and pressed a brief kiss to his cheek. 'You too,' she said, laughing up at him as all around them people hugged and kissed and raised their glasses in toasts.

Conrad grinned. The sexy Aussie was surprisingly great company, effortlessly bringing her out of herself with his sense of humour and his laid-back personality. She'd danced as if no one was watching, laughed at Conrad's improbable tales and drank more beer than she should have drunk given she had to be at work in seven hours. She'd even thrashed Conrad in a highly contested game of England versus Australia darts.

'Wanna head home?' he asked, his hands sliding from her shoulders. 'We both have work tomorrow, and you said you have to be up at five.'

Zara nodded, knocked sideways by his thoughtfulness and by their chemistry that had been simmering away all night. Despite her first impressions of him as a Jack the Lad, he hadn't once crossed the line. There'd been plenty of touching while they'd danced, some flirtatious looks, lots of laughter. But now she wondered if she'd imagined his interest. She was so out of practice when it came to members of the opposite sex. She almost wished Sharon were there for advice. Perhaps he didn't fancy her the way she fancied him. Perhaps he just needed a friend.

Zara blinked, sobered by the memory of his grief earlier when he'd told her about his brother. Now his locum job there, so far from home, made sense. There must be a part of him running away from the pain, the memories, the grief. But those realisations brought more questions, like why he didn't date and why his relationship with his sister-in-law was so tense.

At their table, they collected their hats and coats before spilling out of the pub into the sub-zero temperatures. 'That was so much fun,' she said. 'Thanks for dragging me along. I can't remember ever having such a good time at the local pub.' Despite her earlier reluctance, part of her didn't want such a great night to end.

'You're welcome,' he said. 'All we need now is the fireworks.' He looked up at the clear night sky dotted with stars, before flashing her a cheeky grin that set her pulse aflutter and left her wondering if her life did indeed lack a certain spark. 'Although I guess that's expecting a bit too much.'

'I think so,' she agreed with a chuckle.

They walked in silence for a few minutes, their breath misting the cold, damp air, close, but not too close. After all the touching on the dance floor, the 'happy new year' hug, the way he'd helped her into her coat, Zara missed the contact. Through her own actions, she'd been starved of intimate touch for over five years. As Sharon often pointed out, she'd shut herself off from relationships. Because they were a low priority? Yes. Because she'd had her trust damaged? Probably. Because she was desperately trying to make up for her mistake by being everything

Zach needed, mother and father? So what if that was the case? It harmed no one.

'You okay?' he asked as they arrived at her cottage.

She nodded feeling as if his casual flirtations, his thoughtfulness and sense of humour had brought her back to life. He was ridiculously hot, a nice guy too, once you looked beneath the surface. Behind those dreamy bedroom eyes of his, the laid-back, good-time attitude hid more complex emotions, but even that called to her. Glancing over at his handsome profile, she'd never been more aware of what she'd denied herself since Zach was born—good times with someone her own age, connection, sex. But she should probably think of him as off limits. Kiss him goodnight and leave it there… So why did that idea send her stomach to her boots?

Conrad pushed open the garden gate and stepped aside. 'After you.' He even pulled out his phone and switched on the torch so she could see the path that bisected the lawn and led to her front door.

This was it. Decision time. Give him a peck on the cheek and say goodnight or go for it? She was so confused. And a bit tipsy. And turned on.

They'd barely made it two or three steps inside the garden when he reached for her arm. 'Wait— I think I saw something move.'

Zara froze, peering into the shadowy blackness of the back garden, her fear muted by the heat from his touch and the protective way he stepped forward, putting his body between hers and danger. It had been so long since someone other than her mum had cared and looked out for her, and this was different somehow. Sexier. Gallant.

'It's probably just a fox,' she whispered, trying to pull herself together. 'We get lots of those here.' She needed to calm down. He was just being considerate. Just because he was sexy, funny and charming and a dedicated doctor, didn't mean she seriously wanted to take flirting to the next level, did she? Could she even remember what the next level was? Perhaps that was exactly why she needed to live a little. Sharon was right...

'No, it was smaller than that,' he said, keeping a protective hold on her elbow as they crept further into the garden.

Zara released a tipsy giggle, enjoying that this urbane Australian who most likely didn't even own a pair of wellies was willing throw himself into the path of whatever beast was lurking in the dark. Then her blood ran cold as realisation struck.

'Billy Boy,' she whispered, her panic instantly full-blown.

'Is that an ex of yours?' Conrad said, standing taller as if fully prepared to face up to some thug in her honour.

Zara shook her head and pressed her lips together as another giggle threatened. But an escaped, much-loved pet was no laughing matter. 'No, it's Zach's pet rabbit. He's always escaping. He has a death wish.' She gripped Conrad's arm. 'We have to catch him before a fox does. Zach will be devastated if anything happens to Billy Boy.'

Stepping cautiously onto the frosty grass, Zara walked underneath the house's security-light sensor, triggering a blinding halogen beam that flooded the garden in light. From the corner of her eye, she spied a flash of movement, a blur of grey against the greenery.

'There.' She hurried towards the rabbit, cornering it behind a bush. Conrad stood at the opposite end of the hedge, his stare alive with excitement and amusement, as if he was enjoying himself as much as when they'd danced and played a very competitive game of darts.

'Don't laugh,' she chided, her own lips twitching. 'We need to catch him before he escapes into the fields, or my life won't be worth living.'

'Right.' Conrad nodded, his expression falling serious, which somehow made Zara want to laugh even more.

'Ready?' Zara shook the branches of the hedge to flush Billy Boy out.

The rabbit hopped sedately from his hiding place, utterly unaware of the dangers out in the dark. Zara crouched low, her hands out in front, ready to intercept the fluffy bundle. But before she could get within grasping distance, Conrad dived onto his stomach, his arms outstretched like a rugby player landing a try. His hands closed around thin air. Billy Boy hopped away, evading them both.

Zara burst out laughing, her mirth momentarily outweighing her concern for the pet. She fell back onto her backside with laughter, the dampness from the grass soaking through her jeans.

'What was that?' she asked, tears running down her cheeks as Conrad climbed to his feet and brushed the wet grass from his front.

'I've never caught a rabbit before,' he said, seemingly delighted that he'd made her laugh so hard. 'They're a pest in Australia. Farmers shoot them.'

'Shh,' she hissed, scrambling to her feet. 'He'll hear you.' With her hand on Conrad's arm, they followed the rabbit deeper into the recesses of the garden.

'This time, stay low but nimble,' she instructed Conrad, impervious to the cold because she was enjoying herself so much. 'I normally have to catch him all by myself with Zach too busy giggling to help out.'

Conrad nodded, mock serious. 'So what's the plan this time? Do I catch him while *you* giggle?'

Zara held in another bubble of laughter. She liked that he could laugh at himself, and she'd pay good money to see this tall, sun-kissed Australian catch a pet rabbit in the dark, muddy garden alone. Suddenly his attractiveness tripled.

'I'll flush him out,' she said, trying to be serious, 'and one of us just grabs him. He's not actually that fast because he's a bit over-loved and overfed.'

Conrad limbered up by bouncing on the balls of his feet and shadow-boxing like a like a prizefighter. Zara rolled her eyes and hid another smile, picking her way silently to the far side of the rabbit hutch. She crouched down to find Billy Boy happily munching on a patch of dandelion leaves that had somehow survived the cold. She tried to reach for him but he was already spooked by Conrad's unorthodox belly-dive. He darted away, Zara's fingertips grazing his fur, but he hopped straight into the waiting hands of a very smug Conrad.

'Just like catching a baby,' he said as he stood, a triumphant smile stretching his sexy mouth.

Zara breathed a sigh of both relief and longing. He was far too gorgeous and confident for his own good. And now that Billy Boy was safe, all she could think was how much she wanted to kiss him. Properly.

'Well done,' she said. 'We'll make a rabbit wrangler out of you yet.' She looked away from his victorious expression, his eyes dancing with merriment and something else she wasn't sure she was ready to see: desire.

Did she really want anything to happen between them? Would sleeping with him be reckless? Or just a safe, fun way to explore something she'd denied herself for far too long?

Ignoring the excited flutter in her stomach, Zara opened the hutch and grabbed a handful of fresh straw, shoving it inside Billy Boy's bedroom. While Conrad placed the bunny back inside and closed the door, Zara inspected the cage, finding a corner where the chicken wire had come loose. She stretched the wire over the makeshift nail she'd hammered in the last time the bunny had escaped, reclosing the gap. Tomorrow, after work, she'd dig out a hammer and repair the hutch properly.

'So it's not just pensioners' bingo that gets pulses racing around here,' Conrad said playfully as they headed towards the door to his flat.

Zara smiled up at him, her own pulse still leaping at the power of his sexy smile and the awoken urges pounding through her body. 'We only bring out the escaped bunnies for people who are rubbish at darts,' she said dryly.

He laughed, tossing back his head. Smiling at each other, they paused under the security light beside his door.

'Thanks for tonight,' she said, her voice a little croaky with lust. 'It will be a long time before I'll forget that hilarious rugby dive.'

'You're welcome.' He grinned wider. 'It's nice to see you laugh; you should do it more often.'

Zara stilled, embarrassed by how right he was and by how much she'd neglected her own needs to focus on Zach. No, that wasn't fair. It wasn't Zach's fault. It was fear that had held her back. Fear to be vulnerable with another man after Lorenzo. Of course her son would always be the most important person in her life, but maybe the universe was trying to tell her that it was okay to act her age and have a good time. And she didn't have to be vulnerable with Conrad, not when it could be for just one night.

'Well…goodnight, Zara,' he said when she stayed silent and unmoving for too long. 'Any time you need help catching Billy Boy, just give me a shout.' He leaned close, gripped her shoulder and pressed a cold kiss to her cheek.

Zara's breath trapped in her chest, her heart bounding as his lips lingered on her skin. It was now or never. If she didn't do something right that second, she would always regret it. Before he pulled back, she turned her face and grazed his lips with hers in the merest brush of a kiss.

Conrad peered down at her intensely, his hand on her shoulder still holding her in place. They stared, one second stretching into another, a loaded moment of possibility.

'Sorry,' Zara whispered, uncertain after being so rusty at flirtation for so long. But something had shifted between them, a crackle of awareness. Surely he'd felt it too, this chemistry between them, there all night, just waiting for one of them to acknowledge it? If she was going to put herself out there again, Conrad was as safe a bet as any. He knew her situation, her priorities. Like her, he wasn't looking for a relationship, and he'd be going back to Australia in a few weeks.

'Are you?' he asked, simply, his voice husky and his stare unwavering. 'You shouldn't be.'

She shook her head. 'I'm not really. I'm just aware that I'm seriously back-pedalling. This afternoon at work, I said I wasn't interested in being your next casual conquest. I kind of regret that now.'

She tried to smile and he cupped her cold cheek, his thumb grazing her cheekbone. 'I don't recall that conversation. And life is too short for regrets.'

She flushed, nodding because he was right. 'You can probably tell I don't do this very often...' She couldn't make her feet move away, but was this, kissing him properly, perhaps sleeping with him, a stupid idea? With them practically living together and definitely working together, there'd be no escaping him for the few weeks he was in town. But it was only one night. Just casual sex. What had he called it that first day they met? *No big deal?* If only she was brave enough, it could be the perfect end to a New Year's Eve party unlike any other.

'You haven't done anything yet,' he pointed out, his stare dipping to her lips, as if he wanted more. 'No one is keeping score, Zara. I fancy you. If you fancy me, we could have a good time, nothing serious. Just for tonight if you like.'

He made it sound so easy. She *did* fancy him, and right then 'a good time, nothing serious' was *all* she wanted, *all* she could think about. 'I do want that,' she whispered, her body dragged down with relief and lust.

With an intense stare, he cupped her face in both his hands. 'And I've wanted to kiss you all evening.'

With a jolt of action on both sides, their lips collided in a rush. Conrad wrapped his arms around her and dragged her body flush to his. His lips parted, coaxing her mouth open, and their tongues touched. So turned on she thought she might pass out right there in the frozen garden, Zara kissed him harder, deeper, her hands finding and gripping his hips as she surged onto her tiptoes to keep their lips in contact.

He crushed her mouth under his, a sexy little grunt sounding in his throat as their tongues slid together, back and forth. Zara shut down her thoughts, closed her eyes and surrendered to the hormonal rush. The uninhibited excitement of feeling attractive again, kissing a sexy man who treated her with respect and made her laugh. She spent her every waking moment caring for other people—Zach, her patients, the babies she delivered. She deserved something that was just for her, didn't she? To start the new year off differently from the previous five—with a promise to take better care of herself and her own needs going forward.

Conrad pulled back, his hands still cupping her frozen face, his fingers restlessly sliding into her hair. 'Come inside. It's freezing.'

Zara nodded. He put the key in the lock, ushering her into the cosy, warm flat she'd worked hard to renovate. Before he could speak again, perhaps to offer her a drink or take her coat, Zara turned and kissed him once more, now drunk on the idea that tonight was about sex. He was used to that. Probably good at it, too. And she'd been without it for far too long, as if punishing herself for that one mistake in recklessly choosing Zach's father.

But she wasn't a naive twenty-year-old any more. She was a woman. She knew what she wanted and what she didn't want. And she wanted Conrad.

With his lips on hers, Conrad removed her hat and pushed her coat from her shoulders. His kisses drove her wild and made her forget her responsibilities and the habitual way she kept men at arm's length. Zara caressed his tongue with hers, unbuttoning his coat and reaching for his belt, frantic now that this was really going to happen.

'Are you sure?' he asked when he'd yanked his mouth from hers, his breathing ragged as he pulled her close.

Zara nodded, abandoning his belt buckle as another moment of doubt crept in. 'Although I haven't done this in a very long time, but you've heard about my famous dry spell.' She shrugged, smiled, trying to keep the light playful vibe between them going, because it was a major part of her attraction to him.

'Should I ask how long?' he said, his eyes searching hers while his hands slid restlessly up and down her arms as if he couldn't *not* touch her.

'Since before Zach was born,' she admitted, her high from their kisses dimming slightly.

'Really?' he asked, incredulous, cupping her cheek. 'You're so sexy. It's hard to imagine you're not beating off Englishmen with a stick.'

Zara chuckled, grateful that even now, when part of her was besieged by nerves, he could make her laugh. Then she sobered. 'We should probably keep this between us, though. No one at work needs to know, right?'

Zara didn't want her night with the sexy Australian doctor to be gossip fodder on the maternity ward, not when she was so famously single. Sharon, in particular, would read far too much into it, and it was just one night…

'I hate secrets,' he said, his eyes hardening slightly, 'but this is our business, Zara.' As if sealing the promise with a kiss, he tilted her face up and lowered his lips to hers.

She had no time to wonder why he hated secrets, because this kiss was different, slower, deeper, more determined and thorough, as if it was leading somewhere she definitely wanted to go. Thank goodness she'd shaved her legs in the shower earlier, although her underwear was decidedly practical and no frills, but hopefully it wouldn't be on long enough that he'd notice.

When he slid his lips down the side of her neck and scooped his arm around her waist, pressing her restless body to his hardness, she couldn't hold in her moan. Then they were on the move, her hand clasped in his as he strode to the bedroom. Zara took a split second to notice that he'd changed the sheets since last week, these ones dove grey, not the original snowy white ones, before she gave herself fully over to the thrill and heat of their chemistry.

'You are *so* sexy,' he said, dragging her close once more, his hands in her hair. One hand slid under her jumper to the small of her back and she shuddered under his deep, drugging kisses. 'I promise I'll make this good for you, given you've waited so long,' he whispered against her lips, not that Zara was in any doubt. This was already the best sexual experience of her life and he'd barely touched her yet. But where Lorenzo had been a boy, barely out of his teens, Conrad was a man.

'Okay,' she said, pulling at the hem of his sweater until he yanked it off and threw it aside. His bronzed and defined naked torso called to her hands, so she indulged herself, sliding her palms over his abs, across the mounds of his pecs and the rounded muscles of his shudders. He was indeed all man. Strong and lean. Making her feel small.

Her fingers slid into his hair, and she craned herself up on her tiptoes to kiss him again, her desire flaring to an inferno of need she had no hope of fighting. They kissed, stripping, laughing at a stubborn jeans button and a welded-closed bra clasp. Even the serious business of getting naked was somehow fun with Conrad.

When they stood before each other in just their underwear, he scooped his arms around her waist and tumbled them both onto the bed with a chuckle that turned into a groan.

'I'm so glad you wanted this as much as me.' His hands skimmed her body, his lips, the heat of his breath, trailing over her skin. 'After our first meeting when I thought you seriously meant me harm, it could have so easily gone the other way.'

Zara smiled despite the way his touch inflamed her entire body. 'Never mess with a mama bear defending her den.'

'I wouldn't dream of it.' He slid her body under his, limbs tangled, his body heat scalding, his hands in her hair as his tongue surged against hers. 'And you are one seriously hot mama bear.'

Zara sighed, completely surrounded by and immersed in him, his sexy scent on her skin, the rasp of his facial hair against her chin, encircled in the flexing strength of his toned body. Finally she could relax and surrender, safe in the knowledge that they only wanted this from each other. No relationship, no feelings, no consequences.

He cupped her breast, his thumb rubbing the

nipple erect, and she gasped, holding him closer, hooking one leg over his hip, her pelvis bucking against the hard length of his erection.

'Conrad,' she moaned as he dipped his head and captured the same nipple with his mouth. She was insane with want, scorched with heat, already so close to climaxing. Frantic to have more of him, Zara shoved at his boxers and slid her hand between their bodies, wrapping her fingers around him so he groaned into their kiss. He pulled back, kneeled beside her and removed her underwear, reaching for a condom from his jeans and tossing it onto the bed.

He gazed down at her naked body and Zara had a moment of self-consciousness. She wasn't a tanned, toned pin-up like him. She was an English rose, pale, and had stretch marks, her boobs less perky thanks to breastfeeding Zach. But Conrad didn't seem to care. His stare moved over her nakedness as an art fan admired a Constable. He cupped her breast, slid his hand over her waist and hip and then stroked between her legs.

Zara gasped at his slow, thorough touch. Her heavy stare latched to his as he watched her reactions, learning what made her moan and gasp and reach for him. When he lay beside her, Zara turned to kiss him, her hand finding him once more so they pleasured each other, face to face, hot breath mingling in between heated kisses.

But Zara had waited too long for this degree of intimacy to hold out. His touch infected her entire body in a wave of heat and longing and paralysing bliss that she welcomed, craved, needed.

'You're close,' he said, brushing his lips over hers, his fingers moving between her legs as he peered down at her with that confidence she should find arrogant but only found wildly attractive.

She nodded, impressed that he knew, moaned louder as he captured one nipple with his mouth and sucked. Lights flashed behind Zara's eyes, but then he shifted on top of her and handed her the condom. She tore it open, desperate to have him inside her. She rolled it onto him, fumbling in her haste because he continued to kiss her and stroke her, driving her closer to the edge.

Finally, he scooped his arm around her waist and hauled her under him. Zara panted, parted her legs and then he was kissing her and pushing inside her, so all she could do was cling to him and hold on tight as wonderful pleasure consumed her.

'You okay?' He paused, staring down at her as he pushed her wild hair back from her flushed face and brushed her lips with his.

'Don't stop,' she said, begging, gripping his broad shoulders, her fingertips digging into his steely muscles. Zara crossed her ankles in the small of his back and he sank lower, started to move, watching her reactions in between deep, drugging kisses as if ensuring she was there with him on this journey to oblivion.

'Yes,' Zara said as he gripped her hip and thrust harder, faster. She tunnelled her fingers into his hair and met the surges of his tongue in her mouth with her own, her body pure sensation, her every nerve ending alive, poised on the brink of ecstasy.

Then she was falling, shattered, her body awash with heat and wave after wave of pleasure as her orgasm struck, and she cried out his name in confirmation of the best sex of her life.

Conrad groaned as he picked up the pace, his hips jerking erratically now as he chased his own release. Zara kissed him once more, desperate that this be as good for him as it was for her. With a final jerk, he tore his lips from hers and crushed her tighter, his body taut and his groan muffled against the side of her neck.

She lay under him, panting, coming to her senses. Finally, he rolled sideways, each of them staring up at the ceiling and laughing, while they caught their breath.

'I can't believe I put that off for so long,' she said, her voice full of wonder and euphoria. Had she denied herself sex all these years because she'd been determined to make good on her mistake and be the best mother she could possibly be? Because she was scared to be vulnerable with another man in case she was, once again, rejected? But sex with Conrad was different. Freeing. Truly strings-free.

'That was something else,' Conrad said, tugging her close to press his lips to her temple. '*You* are something else, Zara Wood.'

Zara propped herself up on one elbow, beyond pleased with herself. 'So is this part where you kick me out and I do the walk of shame?' She grinned, enjoying that there was no overthinking to do, no bone-deep trepidation that he might not want to see her again, that he might not want a relationship with her, because *she* didn't want one with *him*.

'You can leave if you want.' He smiled, pressed a kiss to lips and then climbed from the bed and stalked naked to bathroom to take care of the condom. 'But if you give me a few minutes,' he said, casting her a cheeky wink over his shoulder, 'I'd like to do that again.'

'Okay,' she said, watching his toned backside disappear into the en suite before falling back against the pillow with a delighted chuckle.

'Happy new year,' she whispered to herself, hugging her secret close. One day, when Conrad had gone back to Australia, she'd confess to Sharon that she'd finally broken her dry spell. And it had been totally worth the wait.

CHAPTER SIX

ON MONDAY, Conrad arrived at the hospital's out-patient department for an antenatal clinic, his stare scanning the name board for which mid-wives were present that morning. Seeing Zara's name, he felt his pulse bound violently with anticipation.

When he'd woken up New Year's Day morning, Zara had gone, leaving behind only the scent of her perfume on his pillow. Thanks to their differing shifts, and a series of emergency surgeries that had kept Conrad away from the wards and in Theatre, he hadn't seen her since. But a little distance was a good thing. A chance to process what had been, at least for Conrad, an unexpected and seriously hot night.

Entering his designated clinic room, he logged on to the computer and brought up his list of patients to take his mind off Zara. He'd just started to read the notes of the first patient on his list when there was a knock at the door.

'Come in,' he called, looking up from the computer.

The door opened and Zara appeared. Before his instantaneous smile had formed, before he could open his mouth to speak again, the urge to kiss her slammed into him and stole his breath.

'Hi,' he said, his heart rate going nuts. 'Good to see you.' If he'd thought she was sexy before, now that he knew how hot they were together, he really wanted to see her again. They had a great time together. They shared a career and understood the demands of each other's jobs and neither of them wanted a relationship. For him, it didn't get any better than that. But now wasn't the time to raise the possibility.

'You too,' she said, sounding detached. 'Do you have a second to discuss a patient?' She made eye contact but he could tell her guard was back up as if New Year's Eve hadn't happened.

'Of course.' He stood and beckoned her inside.

She entered and left the door ajar, telling him this conversation would definitely be patient-related and in no way personal. 'I've just seen a thirty-four-year-old primip following her twenty-week scan,' she said. 'The placenta is low lying, and she has type one von Willebrand's disease.'

Conrad nodded. 'Thanks for bringing this to my attention. It sounds as if I should see her myself today. She'll need repeated scans,' he went on, outlining an action plan. 'The placenta previa might correct itself as the baby grows, but the bleeding disorder certainly complicates the risks for the mother.'

Placenta previa, when the placenta blocked the opening of the uterus, was enough of a risk of haemorrhage without adding in an inherited blood-clotting disorder in the mother.

'Yes, that's what I thought,' she said, her concern obvious. 'I'll warn you now, before you see her—she's keen to have a home birth.'

'That complicates things.' Conrad winced. This pregnancy definitely qualified as high risk. 'Okay, let's go examine her.'

In Zara's clinic room, he introduced himself to her patient, Helen, and quickly examined the woman's abdomen to confirm the foetal growth matched the scans and corroborated the baby's due date, but everything seemed in order.

'Okay,' he said as the patient adjusted her clothing. 'As I'm sure Zara has explained, your scan shows that the baby is healthy and developing normally. But the scan also shows that the placenta has attached in a low position, near the internal opening of the womb.'

Helen frowned, worry tightening her mouth as she looked between him and Zara. 'What does that mean for my birth plan?'

Conrad drew in a deep breath, preparing to

offer the patient news that might be poorly received. 'Well, the first thing we need to do is monitor your pregnancy a little more closely than we normally would. Sometimes, as the baby grows and the uterus grows too, the position of the placenta can elevate. I'd like you to have another scan in ten weeks' time.'

'Okay,' Helen said, looking relieved.

Zara shot him another meaningful look, full of encouragement, and Conrad nodded, their silent communication telling him they had the same concerns. Part of their job was to try and facilitate the patient's choice when it came to the birth of their child, but their job also involved explaining all of the potential difficulties.

'That being said,' he continued, 'the main risks of a low-lying placenta, which, by the way, affects one in every two hundred pregnancies, is premature labour and haemorrhage, which would obviously be complicated by your inherited bleeding disorder. If the placenta stays where it is, blocking the birth canal, the baby's exit route, I'm afraid I'll be recommending a planned caesarean section around thirty-seven weeks for your safety and that of the baby.'

Tears built in Helen's eyes. Zara passed her a box of tissues, nodding at Conrad in emotional support.

'I understand it's a lot to process, right now,'

Conrad said, hating that he'd made the patient cry, 'but no decisions need to be made today. As I said, the situation could change. Do you have someone you want to call, to meet you here? A support person?'

Helen shook her head, sniffing into the tissue. 'My husband is working in Scotland at the moment.'

Zara rested a comforting hand on the woman's shoulder. 'What about a friend or other relative?'

'My sister actually works in this hospital as a medical secretary,' Helen said, looking up at them.

Conrad nodded encouragingly. 'Why don't you give her a ring? Maybe she could meet you in the café upstairs. They do a wicked scone, and the tea is strong.' He smiled, and Helen laughed through her tears.

'Thank you, Doctor. Thank you, both. I will call my sister. A cup of tea and a scone sounds wonderful.'

Zara shot him a grateful smile he enjoyed way too much.

'Remember,' Conrad said to Helen in parting, 'the most important thing is that the baby is healthy and growing well. Our job—' he glanced at Zara, including her in his statement '—is to present you with all the information so you're aware of all the options and to help you deliver your baby as safely as possible.'

Before he left, his own list of patients calling, Zara looked up from comforting Helen. *Thanks*, she mouthed, her stare glimmering with respect.

He smiled, grateful that that night hadn't altered their working relationship. They were so attuned, so professionally supportive. He'd never worked with anyone quite like Zara. Surely she couldn't ignore their chemistry? Surely she still wanted him the way he wanted her? If not, he would, of course, respect her decision. But with a busy clinic to get through, he'd have to bide his time to ask the question.

Mid-morning, Zara had just added hot water to her instant coffee in the outpatient's break room, when she grew aware of someone at her side. She looked up to see Conrad smiling down at her.

Their eyes locked, and her stomach knotted with giddy anticipation, the same feeling she'd carried since waking up in his bed in the early hours of New Year's Day. Since then, she'd lived on tenterhooks, craving the gorgeous sight of him like a drug but scared to run into him on the ward in case anyone, mainly Sharon, noticed something was different between them.

'Hi, again,' she said, stepping aside to allow him access to the kettle.

'I thought you might like to know that I transferred Jane Phillips to the postnatal ward from HDU last night,' he said, reaching for a spare mug. 'I'm pleased to say that she's doing much better.'

'That's great news,' Zara said in a breathy-sounding voice, nervously glancing over her shoulder, only to discover they had the break room to themselves. 'Thanks for keeping me updated.'

He was such a good doctor, dedicated and compassionate. That he knew she'd be worried about their post-partum haemorrhage patient and wanted to reassure her also spoke to the kind of man he was—caring, intelligent and funny. Now that she knew him better, she saw so much more than a hot guy out for a good time. She saw the doctor who struggled to break bad news to patients because he obviously cared. She saw the man grieving for his brother and missing his young nephew. She saw someone perhaps hiding from something and wondered how she could help him the way he supported her.

'So, how are you?' he asked, his voice low. 'We've managed to somehow accidentally avoid each other since New Year's. But I've been thinking about you.'

'I'm good. Just busy,' she said, stirring her

drink with a trembling hand. 'Never a dull moment around here...'

'True,' he said, that intense interest in his eyes, as if she might be the only woman in the world. 'But I wasn't talking about work. I wondered if you're free for lunch, after clinic? I think we should talk about what happened between us.'

'Talk?' she said, her pulse flying. What was there to say? That she couldn't stop thinking about him either? That she couldn't forget their night together.

'Yes, talk.' He smiled, and she lost her train of thought. 'I'd like to know if you had a good time. Make sure you have no regrets. I don't want us to tiptoe around each other for the next few weeks.'

'I don't have any regrets,' she said, her stare drawn to his mouth. He was awesome at kissing. 'What about you?' Her question emerged as an embarrassing choked whisper.

'None whatsoever, Zara. In fact, I'd like to see you again, perhaps when Zach next sleeps over at your mother's place. I thought we could explore Derby, maybe go dancing. Plus I've been dying to know if Billy Boy is okay after his escape.'

At his mention of the rabbit, Zara laughed, her nerves settling. 'Zach's with my mum Friday, but... I don't know, Conrad. It was supposed to be one night. Zach is still my priority.'

She glanced at the door, worried they'd be interrupted. Worried that someone would be able to tell they were no longer just colleagues. But she was sorely tempted to say yes. They could extend their *nothing serious* into a temporary fling until he left for Australia. What better way to get her confidence back? After all, she wasn't looking for a relationship right now, but she didn't want to be alone for ever.

'Of course he is,' Conrad said with a casual shrug. 'I wouldn't expect anything else. As you know, I'm heading back to Australia in a few weeks. I'm not suggesting we date. I don't really do that any more.'

'Why don't you date any more?' Had someone broken his heart? She'd assumed he was running away from his grief, but maybe it was heartbreak that had chased him from Australia.

He glanced away, looking uncomfortable, and Zara shook her head. 'Sorry, forget I asked. It's none of my business.'

Just because they'd developed a close, supportive working relationship, just because they'd had sex, didn't mean he owed her anything. And the hospital was the last place they could talk.

Conrad inhaled deeply. 'Maybe I'll tell you some time, away from work. Look, I had a good time New Year's Eve, that's all. I got the impression you did too.'

'I did.' She nodded, her body turning instantly

molten with that thrilling need he'd brought back to life on New Year's Eve.

'So, if you wanted to have some more good times, nothing serious, same as New Year's, I'd be interested.' He smiled and she got lost in his eyes for a second. 'I enjoy your company. You have a great sense of humour. It's been a long time since I could laugh with a woman.' He shot her a hopeful smile.

'I enjoy your company, too,' she said, still hesitant. 'But I'll have to pass on lunch, I'm afraid. One of the midwives on the delivery suite today has gone home sick, so I'm heading upstairs after clinic to cover.'

A small frown of disappointment tugged at his mouth. 'Okay, but make sure you grab something to eat. We've had a busy morning down here, and it sounds like you're headed into a busy afternoon.' He looked at her in *that* way. As if, in that moment, she was all he saw.

'I will.' Zara nodded, touched that despite being busy, despite their one night being nothing serious, he cared about *her*. It had been a long time since anyone had put her first. She even put herself last, although she couldn't blame anyone else for that. 'And about Friday…' She glanced at the door, still balanced on a knife edge of indecision. She could almost hear Sharon yell, *Go for it, woman!* And it wasn't as if it could go anywhere. He was leaving in a few weeks and neither of them wanted a serious relationship.

'No pressure,' he said. 'You don't have to answer now. Just think about it.'

Just then Sharon bustled into the room, complaining to no one in particular about the shortage of midwives on duty. Zara stepped away from Conrad, taking a guilty gulp of her scalding coffee and desperately trying to act normal in front of her friend.

'Hi, Sharon,' Conrad said, picking up his own drink. He shot Zara one last glance she prayed Sharon hadn't seen and then left the break room.

'What were you two whispering about?' Sharon asked, flicking on the kettle. The woman never missed a trick.

'Nothing. Just discussing a patient.' It wasn't a lie, exactly, more of an omission. 'Jane Phillips has been transferred off HDU.'

'That's good. How was your weekend?' her friend asked, pouring hot water onto a teabag in a mug. 'Did you do anything for New Year's in the end?' Sharon had invited her to a party at her house, but she'd declined, knowing there would most likely be some single man there that Sharon would tactlessly thrust upon Zara.

She flushed, kicking herself that she hadn't anticipated questions and planned answers that didn't come with revealing blushes. 'Not much. I was working New Year's Day.'

'You should have come over to ours,' Sharon said, stirring her tea. 'Rod invited some people from work. One of them is a lovely guy your age. Smart. Good job. Works in the IT department.' She took a sip of tea and watched Zara over the rim of her mug. 'Want his number?'

'Sharon…' Zara sighed, busying herself with adding another splash of milk to her coffee to cool it down. Perhaps she should take the guy's number just to shut her friend up.

'Don't give me that,' Sharon said. 'It's not healthy always being alone.'

Zara tried not to think about New Year's Eve and Conrad. 'I'm not alone. I have Zach.'

'You know what I mean.' Sharon huffed impatiently. 'You're twenty-six, Zara. You should stop putting your needs last and take better care of yourself. Most people your age are at it like rabbits.'

Zara snorted and flushed again. She'd waited five years to let a man close enough for intimacy, but now that she had, all she could think about was Conrad and his mad bedroom skills. And he wanted to see her again…

'It's not the sex that puts me off,' she admitted. 'It's just—'

'I know. You've been hurt, so you struggle to trust men.'

Zara looked up sharply. Her friend wasn't wrong. What would she say if she knew Zara was denying herself more casual sex with the department hottie, just because, since Lorenzo, ignoring men had become a bad habit?

Sharon's expression brimmed with sympathy. 'Not all men are selfish and irresponsible, you know.'

'I know that,' Zara said, wondering how, despite all her tough talk and fierce independence, she'd allowed Conrad to charm his way under her defences.

'I know that you're focussed on raising Zach. I know you want the best for him, as if you're making up for his lack of a father, but it's important that you're happy too.'

'You're right.' Zara nodded, unable for once to argue. She had been putting her own needs last. And if Conrad was willing to wait for her, to snatch chances to be with her when Zach was at her mother's, she'd be a fool to pass that up, wouldn't she? 'Would it make you feel any better to know I've made a new year's resolution to take better care of myself going forward?'

A brief fling with Conrad was a perfect temporary situation, as if the universe had dropped a sexy, single toy into her lap. She should take

what was on offer—a good time, nothing serious—and simply enjoy a long-overdue sexual
adventure.

'Yes,' Sharon said, scooping up her mug and
following Zara from the break room. They
needed to get back to work.

'Then stop worrying,' Zara said, pausing outside her clinic room to shoot her friend a reassuring smile. She was going to do it, to see Conrad
again. And now that she'd made up her mind,
Friday seemed a long way off.

CHAPTER SEVEN

CONRAD HAD JUST finished seeing his final patient of the morning, when there was another knock at the door. 'Come in,' he called, looking up to see Zara poke her head through the opening.

'Zara!' Their eyes locked. 'Come in.' She had her bag over her shoulder so she was obviously headed up to the ward.

'I just wanted to catch you,' she said breathlessly, her eyes bright with excitement. 'I've thought about it and my answer is *yes*.'

Conrad stood and came around to her side of the desk, unable to dampen his smile. 'That's fantastic. So we can do something Friday?'

She nodded and stepped close, her pupils dilating. Realisation dawned, his heart rate spiking. She had *that* look in her eyes. He reached for her at the same moment she hurled herself into his arms. Their lips clashed. He scooped one arm around her back while the other tilted her face up to his deepening kiss.

'Thank goodness you caved,' he said breathlessly after tearing his mouth from hers. 'I've wanted to do this for the past two days.' His lips found hers once more and he pushed her back against the closed door.

'Me too.' Zara gripped his waist and dragged him close. 'But no one can know about this, okay? The gossip would be unbearable.'

'Okay...' Conrad frowned, his mind blanking when she pulled his lips back to hers. 'Although I'm not a fan of secrets.' But his desire for her outweighed everything. And besides, he was only in England for another couple of weeks so did it really matter?

'I know, but if Sharon finds out about us, she'll want to play cupid. The woman is relentless. She's even tried to fix me up this morning with some guy who works with her husband.'

A sudden flare of possessiveness heated his blood.

'And it's not like this can go anywhere,' she continued. 'Neither of us are looking to date and we live in different countries.'

'I can't argue with any of that,' he said. And he couldn't. He cupped her face and brushed her lips with his. 'So you'll meet me Friday, when Zach is at your mum's? Give me something to look forward to.' He kissed the side of her neck, his hand cupping her breast so she sighed, her body sagging against his.

'I'll meet you Friday,' she said, shuddering. 'But it's just sex, agreed?'

Conrad didn't play games. He wasn't making her any promises, but Zara knew what she wanted and, more importantly, what she didn't want. And so did he.

'No arguments from me.' He smiled, reeling when she gripped the lapels of his white coat, pressed a kiss to his lips and then shoved him away.

'I have to go. Until Friday.' She straightened her uniform and reached for the door handle.

'Zara,' he said as she swung the door open. 'I can't wait.' He adjusted the knot of his tie, his heart thumping wildly.

She grinned. Suddenly, it was as if they were transported back to that moment in the garden when they'd laughed together over the escaped rabbit and then kissed, their passion for each other burning quickly out of control.

With a final flirty look, she left. He dragged in a deep breath. It was going to be a very long week.

By nine p.m. Friday, Conrad had just about given up hope that Zara would keep her word, when there was a rap of knuckles on the door. He leapt off the sofa with the eagerness of a kid on Christmas morning and swung open the door, his pulse frantic.

'Hi. You look lovely.'

'Hi.' Zara smiled and hurried inside out of the cold.

No sooner had he closed the door behind her than she hurled herself into his arms, her lips meeting his in a desperate kiss. After days of restless anticipation, of secret looks on the ward and pretending she was just another midwife, her desperation resonated deeply with him.

'That was the longest week of my life,' he said when Zara let him up for air. 'How's Zach, by the way?'

'He's fine. He loves his Friday sleepovers at Grandma's,' she said, shrugging off her coat and immediately tugging at his shirt buttons. 'I want you.' She trailed her lips seductively down the side of his neck, making him groan.

He nodded in agreement, his desire for her as acute as their first time thanks to the build-up. 'What about Derby...dancing?' he asked, half-heartedly putting up a feeble fight.

'Who needs dancing?' she said, her demanding hands everywhere at once: inside his shirt, in his hair, tugging at his neck to bring their lips back together. 'I'm making up for lost time.'

Absorbing every kiss, Conrad stumbled into the nearby lounge where they collapsed onto the sofa together. Truth was, he didn't care one jot about Derby. What could the city really have to offer to rival Zara, naked and playful in his bed? He'd never wanted anyone as much as he wanted her right then.

'Your famous dry spell?' he said with a smile as she sat astride his lap and removed her sweater. Conrad's brain short-circuited at the sight of her amazing breasts clad in the sexy black lace of her bra. He sat up, capturing her lovely lips once more so she shuddered in his arms.

'I can't believe I ignored this side of myself for so long,' she said on a sigh as he popped her bra clasp and leaned forward to capture one of her nipples in his mouth. 'Seeing you at the hospital and not being able to kiss you has been hell.'

'I know,' he said when she tugged his shirt overhead and reached for the button on his jeans. 'I spent the entire week walking around the hospital, looking for secret places I could lure you. I found a large cleaning cupboard outside the postnatal ward that looked very promising.'

Zara laughed, smiled down at him indulgently. 'Hold that thought. You never know when it might come in handy.'

His laughter died as she shoved him down on the sofa and traced her lips down his chest and his abs, moaning as she unzipped his jeans. Conrad froze, recognising that wicked look in her eyes. When she freed him from his underwear and took him into her mouth he almost passed out, so sharp was the ache of pleasure in his gut. She drove him crazy, the yearning and waiting a sick kind of sensual torture, so that now he was on edge, his stamina shot to pieces as he watched her pleasure him with her mouth.

Then he sprang into action. 'Let's go,' he said, standing and pulling her to her feet. In the bedroom, they stripped off the rest of their clothes with unhurried determination, their stares locked. When they were naked together on the bed, he kissed his way from her lips to her breasts, from her stomach to between her legs. He couldn't seem to get enough of her, or stop touching her, kissing her, relishing her every moan and sigh.

'Conrad.' Zara gasped, her fingers twining restlessly in his hair as she looked down at him, the way he'd watched her. His name on her lips did something to him, something primal and possessive. He wanted to hear it over and over.

'Do you want me as much as I want you?' he asked in the pause for the condom.

'Yes,' she said. 'I tried to fight it, but I don't know what you've done to me. It's as if you've flicked a switch to my libido. I'm suddenly addicted to sex.'

Satisfied, he smiled and lay on top of her, kissing up her cries and moans as his fingers moved between her legs. They were obviously intoxicated by each other. When he finally pushed inside her, the hunger he'd tried to ignore since New Year's Eve consumed him so he had to close his eyes for a second against the rush of desire.

'This is the best sex I've ever had,' she said, pulling his lips down to her kiss, her hips moving against his.

'Me too,' he said, entwining their fingers and pressing her hand into the mattress as he moved over her. She stared up at him with arousal and wonder and joy. He could get used to putting that look on her face, just as he couldn't imagine tiring of the way she made him feel, almost as if he'd been waiting his whole life for a woman like her. But that was crazy and just lust talking. Sex that good could mess with your mind.

He kissed her more thoroughly, moving slowly inside her, drawing out the pleasure until their skin was slicked with perspiration and they were both so desperate for release they finally came together, their mingled cries filling the darkened room. As their hearts banged together, Conrad pressed his lips to hers, struggling to withdraw from the heat of her body and struggling to abandon the dizzying high they generated together. It had been years since he'd felt this connected to a woman, but maybe it was simply because they had so much in common beyond sexual chemistry: their grief, their work, her son and his nephew.

Finally, he rolled onto his back and pulled her under his arm, pressing his lips to her forehead. 'You are the hottest midwife I've ever met. I'm so glad you wanted more than just one night.'

She laughed. 'You, Dr Reed, were simply too much temptation.'

'I've created a monster,' he said, smiling, drawing her lips up to his.

When she laughed, he couldn't help but kiss her again.

Afterwards, Conrad switched on some chilled music and padded through to the kitchen naked, returning to bed with two large glasses of red wine.

'Do you mind that we didn't go to Derby?' Zara asked, taking one and placing it on the bedside table.

'Of course not.' He joined her in bed, tilted up her chin and brushed her lips with his. 'I seriously doubt there's anything in the city that's anywhere close to as great as what we just did.'

'You're not wrong.' Zara chuckled, her laughter turning to fear when he reached for her hand under the duvet. Holding his hand felt way too natural and somehow more intimate than all the other things they'd done. But relying on each other at work, supporting each other emotionally through the tricky cases, made this connection between them understandably intense. It didn't mean anything. It couldn't.

'Can I ask you something?' she said, to distract herself from those confusing thoughts.

'Of course,' he said, slinging his arm around her shoulders.

'You said you don't date any more. You said you'd tell me why,' she said, snuggling into his side. 'Did someone break your heart?'

He stilled and sighed, giving her a glimpse into his feelings on the subject. 'I was in love once, a long time ago. But I moved too fast and she didn't feel the same way, so she broke up with me. Since then, I've kept things casual.'

Zara pressed a kiss to his chest over the rapid thump of his heart. 'I'm sorry you were hurt, Conrad.'

'Don't worry.' His arm tightened around her. 'I'm over it. What about you?' he asked, switching the focus. 'You're twenty-six and a complete bombshell. Did Zach's father break *your* heart?'

Zara laughed and looked up, her ego preening. 'Bombshell, eh? I'll have to remember that compliment next time I'm cleaning out Billy Boy's hutch in my wellies.'

Conrad smiled softly, clearly waiting for a real answer.

'I wouldn't say he broke my heart as such. His name was Lorenzo,' she said, her stomach twisting with embarrassment. 'I was so young when I met him, and very naive. It wasn't a great love story, just a holiday fling—exciting, intense, exotic.'

Her heart raced, her discomfort soothed by the rhythmic slide of Conrad's fingers up and down her arm. 'He said he loved me, but I didn't really believe him,' she went on. 'He worked as a waiter at the Spanish resort where me and my friends were staying. I knew there'd been other foreign girls before me, and there would be more after me.'

'So you weren't that naive, then,' he pointed out. 'Just young and enjoying yourself. There's no harm in that.'

Zara shrugged, dragging in a deep breath, the next part of the story sure to resurface the humiliation she'd felt after her final phone call to Lorenzo. 'When I came home, I'd accepted that we probably wouldn't see each other again, even though we'd swapped phone numbers. Then a couple of weeks later I found out I was pregnant.'

Conrad nodded, urging her to continue.

'I was still in shock myself when I called Lorenzo,' she said, her breathing shallow as she relived the difficult emotions. 'I didn't really know what I expected from him, but it was more than the nothing I received. I figured he might want to come to the UK to meet his child, or ask me to bring the baby to Spain, even if he and I weren't going to be together. But he did none of those things. He got angry when I refused to consider a termination. Said I was a stupid, immature girl and hung up on me.'

Conrad's harsh frown distorted his mouth. '*He* sounds like the immature one, if you ask me. So he let you both down? You and Zach?'

Zara shrugged, feeling a little sick as her protective urges for her son flared up. 'I was upset in the beginning, obviously. I didn't understand how someone could know they had a child in the world and not want to meet them.'

'I couldn't do it,' he said and Zara pressed her lips to his, instinct telling her his assertion was genuine. Where Lorenzo had been a boy, Conrad was a real man.

'Me neither,' she added, wishing she'd made a baby with someone more like Conrad. 'As my pregnancy progressed, I thought he might change his mind once he'd had time to come to terms with it, call one day out of the blue. But he didn't. After a while, I stopped waiting for the phone to ring.'

'I'm so sorry that you had to go it alone. That

must have been hard, especially in the beginning.'

She shook her head, brushing aside his empathy. 'I had both my parents for support initially. And once Zach was born, I focussed on being his mother, on making sure he didn't pay for my recklessness, for a mistake in choosing the wrong father for him.'

Conrad glanced at her sharply. 'Maybe the mistake was Lorenzo's, not yours. After all, you're the one who's been there for your son, every day from before he was born. You carried him, delivered him and raised him, doing the work of two parents.'

Zara shrugged, dismissing his praise, but her heart swelling with maternal pride. 'I'm so lucky. He's a great young man.'

'Maybe it's because he has a great mother,' he said, refusing to allow her to brush him off. 'You know, just because you consider you made a mistake, doesn't mean you need to pay the price for ever. We're allowed to be naive and daring when we're young. To get carried away by our feelings and have intense romances.'

She frowned. Had she decided that raising Zach alone was some sort of penance for making a mistake with Lorenzo? Was that why she'd ignored her own needs for so long?

'You sound like Sharon,' she said, a fresh flutter of anticipation in her stomach. This fling with Conrad had certainly whet her appetite for sex.

'I guess I'm saying that you definitely don't *need* a man,' Conrad continued, turning serious, 'but one day, you might want a relationship. Don't close yourself off to that possibility or put yourself last. You're young. You still have so much living to do, and your happiness is as important as Zach's.'

Zara held her breath, torn. She liked that he cared about her well-being. But she'd spent so long going it alone, she didn't really know how to let someone, a man, that close. Maybe when this fling was over she'd be ready to start dating, for real. But could she find someone who not only wanted her, but also wanted to help her raise Zach? The way her stomach pinched with worry, that seemed like a pretty tall order.

Rather than admit those deep fears, Zara wrapped her arms around Conrad's neck, drawing his mouth down to hers. 'You are such a romantic, Dr Reed.'

'Am I?' he asked, seeming genuinely puzzled.

Zara nodded, wondering anew at the mystery woman who'd broken Conrad's heart. 'Let's hope, one day, we can both move on. Meeting you has certainly shown me that what I really need right now is a wild sexual adventure, the kind I missed out on by becoming a mum relatively young.'

'A wild sexual adventure?' He perked up. 'And that's where I come in, is it?' His expression turned to playful delight as he wrapped his arm around her waist, dragging her under him for a passionate kiss.

'It is.' She nodded and giggled. 'Feel up to the challenge?'

'Oh, I think so.' He grinned, brushed his lips over hers. 'Any time you want secret, late-night sex, you know exactly where to find me.' His hand skimmed her hip and her waist, cupping her breast where his thumb teased her nipple.

As Conrad set about proving that he was indeed the man for the job, Zara lost herself in their playful passion, forgetting all about their exes and past heartaches. As he'd said, life was short and so was this fling. Best to enjoy it while it lasted, because the last thing it could be was for ever.

CHAPTER EIGHT

IT WAS THE start of the following week before Zara saw Conrad again. Her weekend had been filled with the usual mum duties and domestic chores. She'd arrived at work that morning with an extra spring in her step, excited that their paths might cross once more. But there was no time now for goofy grins or sexy daydreams.

Zara had paged Conrad to urgently review an inpatient he'd admitted the day before. The woman, who was at thirty-five weeks' gestation, was being monitored following premature rupture of the membranes, or PROM.

As he marched onto the maternity ward with his SHO, Max, in tow, Zara sighed with relief and quickly intercepted him.

'Dr Reed,' she said. 'I need you to review Mrs Hutchins, the patient you admitted yesterday with pre-term PROM.'

The barely perceptible flicker of heat and recognition in his stare was, of course, gratifying, but it became quickly shrouded in concern and professionalism. They might be very pleased to see each other after days apart, but their patients always came first.

'What's going on?' he asked, pausing outside the patient's room to hurriedly wash and dry his hands.

'Her observations have been stable,' Zara said, bringing him up to speed. 'No sign of labour or infection and she's had her steroids. But this morning, after showering, the patient reported she felt something prolapsing internally. I think it's the umbilical cord. We've confined her to bed and placed her in the head down position to relieve any pressure on the cord.'

Conrad pulled on a face mask, his stare etched with the same concern for the patient that Zara felt. 'How's the foetal heart rate? Any signs of distress?'

Zara shook her head. 'It's stable, too. No bradycardias to report.' But they both knew the risks with premature rupture of the membranes. Infection, premature labour and foetal distress were serious enough compilations. But umbilical cord prolapse or compression could be life-threatening, especially for the baby.

'Okay,' Conrad said with a decisive nod. 'You did the right thing in calling me.' He met her stare, his conveying reassurance and faith. 'Let's take a look.'

They entered the room, where Sharon was with the patient. After greeting Mrs Hutchins, Conrad pulled on sterile gloves. 'I need to examine you, Mrs Hutchins.'

Zara waited nervously, trying to keep her concerns for the patient and her unborn baby from her expression. When he'd finished his examination, Conrad glanced at Zara and gave her a worrying nod of confirmation. 'You're right. It *is* the cord.'

Zara swallowed her fear. She'd never personally come across a case of umbilical cord prolapse before. She'd never been more relived that he was there.

Conrad turned to the patient. 'Mrs Hutchins, that feeling you have of something prolapsing inside is the baby's umbilical cord. It's slipped down outside the uterus. There's a risk that if we leave it, the blood supply to the baby could be compromised. I'm afraid we're going to need to deliver the baby with an emergency Caesarean section today.'

The patient nodded tearfully, her stare full of understandable alarm, but Zara was so grateful for the calm authority in Conrad's voice. She'd found it reassuring, so hopefully the patient had also.

Zara took Mrs Hutchins' hand. 'Try not to worry. The baby is fine at the moment. We just need to deliver him or her quickly and safely, okay?'

'Have you called Mr Hutchins?' Conrad asked Sharon, tossing his gloves in the bin and pulling out his phone while Max took some blood from the patient's arm in preparation for surgery.

'Yes,' Sharon said. 'He's working in Manchester today, so he might be a while. But he's on his way.'

From the corner of the room, Conrad made a quick but hushed call to the obstetrics theatre and the anaesthetist, glancing Zara's way with a concerned stare. She knew what he was thinking: there was no time to wait for the husband. Any shift of the baby's position could compress the cord and interfere with the baby's blood supply.

Having hung up the phone, Conrad addressed the patient once more. 'I'd be happier if we deliver this baby right now, Mrs Hutchins. I don't think we can wait for dad. Better for him to meet the little one safely delivered. Do you agree?'

The woman nodded, and Conrad unlocked the wheels of the bed. Seeing the grip the patient still had on Zara's hand, he met her stare. 'Zara, are you up for a trip to Theatre?'

She shot him a grateful nod and turned to the patient. 'I'll stay with you until your husband arrives.'

'Then let's go have this baby,' Conrad said, his

own expression impressively calm as, together, they wheeled the patient towards the lifts and headed for Theatre.

With relief pounding through his veins following the emergency C-section, Conrad placed the healthy newborn baby girl onto her mother's chest for some immediate skin-to-skin contact.

'Congratulations. You have a daughter.'

As the neonatal nurses hovered nearby, ready to whisk the pre-term baby away for some initial checks and to be weighed, Zara and Mrs Hutchins stared at the newborn in wonder. Conrad's stare met Zara's over the tops of their theatre masks. Tears shone in her eyes, a raft of emotions shifting there—relief, gratitude, respect. Conrad lapped it up, his heart beating wildly that he and Zara could share this special, professional moment.

In a short time, things had gone from terrifyingly urgent to the happiest outcome, the kind their work was renowned for: a safely delivered and healthy baby. But today, maybe because Zara was there with him in Theatre, the rush he normally felt was amplified tenfold.

Yes, this was his job and he and Zara were just having casual sex. But ever since his brother's violent and untimely death, Conrad had become increasingly aware of how quickly life could change. You could lose what you cared about in a heartbeat.

Focussed on the fundal massage of the uterus and the delivery of the placenta, Conrad quietly guided Max through the surgical closure of the uterine incision while Zara and neonatal team cared for the mother and baby. With the surgery complete, he removed his gloves and gown and spoke to the patient, who was now cradling her sleeping baby adoringly.

'We got there a little earlier than planned, but it looks like she's doing really well.' He smiled, loving this part of his job—the end result. 'I hope Mr Hutchins isn't too upset that we started without him.'

'Thank you for delivering her safely, Doctor,' the patient said, her eyes shining with tears as she rested a hand on his arm. 'She's perfect and I'm so grateful to you and the whole team.'

Conrad swallowed, her gratitude catching him off guard for a second, maybe because Zara was present and listening, watching on with shining eyes.

'I'll come and check on you back on the ward,' he said. Before he moved away, he glanced at Zara, who was looking at him every bit as adoringly as Mrs Hutchins. A moment of silent communication and emotional support passed between them.

You did a good job. I couldn't have done it without you. Thank you.

Did she trust him the way he trusted her? It seemed crazy given they'd only known each other a couple of weeks. But maybe the feast or famine nature of their fling, the stolen moments of intimacy they snatched when they could, made every moment, together or apart, more intense. Maybe that explained their building connection.

Reluctantly, he left Theatre, tossing his face mask and disposable hat into the bin before washing up. He was just about to head for the coffee room, where he hoped some much-needed caffeine would settle his thoughts, when he spied Sharon.

'How did it go?' she asked, her frown easing as he nodded his head.

'All good. A textbook C-section. The baby is a bit small, but otherwise seems healthy. Zara is still with them.' He glanced back towards Theatre, as if reluctant to leave without Zara.

Sharon chuckled. 'There was no way Zara was letting go of that woman's hand. She hates not being able to see a delivery through to the end. I swear if she didn't have Zach to care for, some days she probably wouldn't go home at all.'

He nodded. 'She's a great midwife.' And an amazing woman and mother. He hadn't come to England looking for a romantic relationship. He'd come to forget about the twisted love triangle he'd been dragged into by Marcus and Tessa. To grieve for Marcus without the constant reminders of the betrayals of the past. To give Tessa the space she'd requested when he'd tried to be there for James. But there was something about Zara he couldn't help but allow close. Closer than he'd allowed anyone since he'd learned the truth about his brother and his ex.

'She is. I keep telling her what a catch she is,' Sharon said. 'But Zach's father really let them down.'

He smiled, non-committal. He'd been surprised by how much Zara had shared with him last Friday night about her feelings of betrayal, rejection and humiliation. Maybe she was starting to trust him. And like Sharon, it really bothered Conrad that Zara blamed herself for a youthful mistake, when Zach's father had simply walked away without taking any responsibility for his son.

'Are you enjoying working here?' Sharon asked, switching subjects.

'It's great,' he said, with genuine feeling. 'I'm getting lots of experience and more surgical time than in Brisbane.'

'Maybe you should keep your eye open for a consultant post here. There are a couple of older obstetricians who are close to retirement age.'

'Maybe I will,' he said. 'But I'm not in any rush. No point applying for a consultant post until I know where I want to settle.' For now, he couldn't really think beyond going back to fix things with his brother's wife. They were both grieving, but now that Conrad had seen Zara's devotion to Zach, he could understand why Tessa had told him to back off. Perhaps he *had* been overprotective of James at a time when he was still processing his own grief for Marcus.

'See you later,' Sharon said, turning and exiting the department, leaving Conrad wondering how he was going to walk away from Zara when the time came.

Conrad was about to head for a nearby stairwell, when he heard his name being called. Zara caught up with him, wordlessly widening her eyes and tilting her head in the direction of the stairs. With his heart bounding, he followed. The door swung closed at his back, and Zara hurled herself into his arms, her lips clashing with his in a breathy kiss that almost knocked him off his feet.

'That was amazing,' she said, after pulling back to look up at him, her hands gripping his face. 'You are amazing. Thank you for letting me be a part of that delivery.'

Euphoria rushed Conrad's blood. He didn't need her praise, but it felt good to know their professional regard, their trust, was mutual. 'It was a team effort. I couldn't have done it without you, and, as it happens, I think you're amazing, too.' Now his feelings of closeness made sense. Their relationship *was* intense. How could it not be? They were sleeping together, essentially living together and working together.

She smiled, kissed him again, and, despite them being at work, despite the fact that they might be discovered, Conrad couldn't help but kiss her back. He slid his tongue against hers and pressed her up against the closed door as desire hijacked his system.

'How can I want you all the time?' she said, when they came up for air, her body shifting restlessly against his, a reminder of how she felt naked in his arms, her passionate cries ringing out.

Dopamine flooded his brain, swiftly followed by a sense of panic, a desperation to be alone with her once more. Not Friday night, but now.

'Can I see you tonight?' he whispered against her lips in between her desperate kisses. Suddenly, Friday seemed like a long way off. Too long. Clearly his physical need for her had reached uncontrollable levels, otherwise he wouldn't be risking discovery by kissing her at work. But in a couple of weeks, he'd be flying home to sort out his personal life. In the meantime, he wanted as much of Zara as he could get.

'I can't,' she said, with a sigh. 'It's a school night. I... I don't want to confuse Zach.'

Conrad's stomach sank, even though he understood. 'Of course not. I totally understand. I don't want that either.' He'd always known that Zach was her number one priority and he respected her for putting her son first. 'You're a great mother, Zara. I hope you know that.'

He was desperately trying not to judge Tessa's parenting, but a part of him couldn't help but worry that her withdrawal from the Reed family wasn't in James's best interests. Surely the boy needed his father's family, now more than ever. But maybe Tessa needed time to build new routines for her and James, in the same way Zara protected Zach.

'I just can't seem to get enough of you,' he admitted, pushing the hair back from her face and brushing her lips with his, one last time. Then he reined himself back under control as he stepped back, put some distance between their bodies.

'Me neither,' she said, her teeth snagging her bottom lip in a very distracting way. 'Unless...' She hooked her index finger into the V-neck of his scrub top so he couldn't step too far away. 'I could text you once Zach is asleep.' She blinked up at him playfully. 'Perhaps you could tiptoe up for a sneaky glass of wine.'

His pulse went crazy, his need for her outweighing his dislike of *sneaking around*. But he understood her reasons and it wasn't as though *their* clandestine activities were hurting anyone.

'I'd love to, but only if you're sure,' he said. 'Honestly, no pressure. I respect your boundaries. The last thing I want to do is make you feel uncomfortable or confuse Zach.' Not that Zara was ready to introduce the boy to some strange man.

'I'm sure,' she said. 'I'll text you tonight. I'd better get back to Mrs Hutchins.' She smiled, her stare sweeping over him in a way that was full of promise. Then she pulled open the door, blew him a cheeky kiss and disappeared.

Conrad dragged a ragged breath, stunned by the force of his addiction to Zara Wood. But he needed to be careful, to keep his emotions in check the way he'd done since rushing things with Tessa. He couldn't get carried away by their harmonious working relationship and great sex. He didn't want to hurt Zara or get hurt himself, and, as he'd said to Sharon, his life was back in Australia. His one comfort was that Zara seemed to know what she wanted, and it wasn't a real relationship.

CHAPTER NINE

THE NEXT MORNING, as soon as Conrad opened his eyes, a grin stretched his mouth, his first thought of Zara. She *had* texted him last night, once Zach had fallen asleep. They'd shared a bottle of wine by the fire, whispering like a couple of teenagers up late without parental knowledge. Wine had led to kissing, kissing to nakedness after Zara had sneaked him into her bedroom and covered his mouth with her hand to dampen any noise as they'd climaxed together. The clandestine nature of their desperate coupling had made it somehow hotter. Although Zara was almost too hot to handle, just as she was.

Conrad stretched out his body after a great night's sleep and headed for the shower. Given that he was covering the on call that coming weekend, he had today off, but he couldn't just lie around thinking about his favourite midwife. Perhaps he'd go for a walk. Head into the hills around Morholme, get some fresh air and think about what he would say to Tessa when he returned to Australia. Just as he respected Zara's boundaries, he would respect Tessa's, but he still wanted to be a part of James's life.

When he emerged from the bathroom ten minutes later, he heard squeals of laughter from outside. He quickly dressed and opened the curtains. The unexpected sight that greeted him forced out a bark of delighted laughter. The garden, the fields beyond, the surrounding rooftops were all blanketed in a thick layer of snow.

Conrad's pulse picked up with excitement. Aside from a few skiing holidays in New Zealand when he was a teenager, he had little experience of snow. He'd certainly never lived anywhere with cold enough winter temperatures for snowfall.

Just then, a little boy he assumed was Zach ran past his window, his cheeks ruddy from the cold and a pair of multicoloured gloves dangling from the sleeves of his coat by string. Conrad smiled at the boy's infectious joy, imagining how James too would love to play in the snow. A flood of sadness swamped him for all the moments in his son's life that Marcus would miss. It made Conrad all the more determined to patch things up with Tessa when he returned home so he could be there for James, not as a substitute father, but as an uncle who would be there if needed.

Zara appeared and, just like that, Conrad's

sadness lessened. She chased after Zach, her hair caked with powdery snow and her breath misting the air in front of her as she laughed. She hurled a snowball, striking Zach in the back.

Conrad smiled wider. They were obviously having a snowball fight and, with a direct hit to head versus one to the torso, Zach was clearly winning.

In that second, Zara looked up and spied Conrad at the window. He raised his hand in a wave, his pulse galloping as usual as their eyes met. He prepared to move away from the window, reluctant to interrupt their fun. But before he could step back, Zara scooped two handfuls of snow from the ground, formed a tight ball between her palms and threw the snowball in his direction. It struck the window with a thump, right at Conrad's eye level. But for the pane of glass, it would have been a direct hit to the face.

Triumph gleamed in Zara's stare as she laughed, delighted with herself. 'Afraid of a little snow?' she called, beckoning him to join them at the door to the flat.

Conrad headed through to the kitchen and pulled open the door to a rush of frigid air and the crisp scent of fresh snow.

'Conrad,' Zara said, from his doorstep, 'this is Zach.' She looked down at her son. 'Conrad is from Australia.'

Conrad shook the boy's hand. 'Good to meet you, Zach. Looks like you're having a fun time and it seems you're better at snowball fights than your mother.'

'We're building a snowman,' Zach said proudly, stooping to grab another two handfuls of the irresistible powder.

'That sounds awesome. I've never done that.'

'Really?' Zach asked, looking up at him with astonishment.

'I don't think they have snow in Conrad's country,' Zara explained, her eyes full of pitying laughter.

Conrad smiled, pleased to see her, given she was supposed to be at the hospital right now. 'You didn't go into work?' he asked.

She shook her head. 'It's a snow day. School's closed, and the roads out here are impassable. But don't worry, they'll be out with the gritters soon. They'll have the roads cleared by tomorrow. Best to enjoy it while it lasts.'

'Do you want to help us build a snowman?' Zach asked Conrad. 'It's going to be so cool.'

'Good idea.' Zara nodded and ruffled Zach's hair.

Conrad hesitated, reluctant to gatecrash their precious family time. 'Are you sure?' he asked, respectful of her boundaries.

'Definitely,' she said, with a smile. 'Come and play.'

'Okay, thanks, Zach.' Conrad reached for his trainers, which were near the door. 'I'd love to help build a snowman.'

'You'll have soggy feet in seconds wearing those,' Zara said, glancing at the trainers.

'I only have these and my work shoes with me. I didn't pack for snow.' He looked at her feet. She and Zach were wearing gumboots.

'I still have my dad's wellies in the shed.' Zara smiled. 'They might fit you. Let me go grab them.'

While Conrad quickly donned his coat, Zach wandered off to retrieve his yellow plastic spade, the kind you'd take to the beach for building sandcastles. Within seconds Zara returned with boots. Conrad shoved his feet into them and stepped outside. The snow was inches thick, blanketing the entire garden, even the path. He stepped gingerly to avoid slipping, the rubber soles of the boots squeaking against the compacted snow.

'Come on,' she said, urging him to her and Zach's half of the garden where they'd already made a good start on the body of the snowman, a mound taller than Zach.

'Now we can make him even taller, Mum,' Zach said, excitedly patting handfuls of snow onto the mound. He looked up at Conrad. 'How tall are you?'

'I'm six foot two,' Conrad said, reaching for two handfuls of snow. 'Let's see if we can make him taller than me.'

'Yeah,' Zach cheered, enthusiastically piling snow higher and higher as Zara cast Conrad a look full of gratitude.

They threw themselves into the challenge, laughing as the mound grew taller and taller. Within seconds Conrad's fingers were frozen and the cuffs of his coat were damp, but he was having too much fun to care.

'Let's make a giant snowball for the head,' said Zach to Conrad, running to the far end of the garden where the snow was thick and undisturbed.

'Careful, mate, it's slippery on the path,' Conrad called out before he could stop himself.

Zara cast him an amused and curious stare. 'He's fine. Don't worry—he's English. He's made of tough stuff.'

Conrad winced. 'Sorry. I just wouldn't want him to fall and whack his head.'

'Thank you for looking out for him,' she said, her expression softening.

Conrad shrugged, adjusting his thinking as he joined Zach, who was rolling a snowball through the snow to help it grow. Of course, Zach wasn't *his* responsibility, but he couldn't help but be protective of the little guy, who reminded Conrad so much of James he experienced another pang of missing his nephew. Fresh guilt rushed him, because his overprotectiveness had upset Tessa, had contributed to pushing her and James away. He knew that. It was something he would need to fix.

By the time he and Zach returned from their trip around the garden, the snowball head was five times the size of the one they'd started with.

'Ready to put the head on top?' he asked Zach, who nodded and looked up at his mother expectantly.

'Is it okay if I put him on my shoulders?' Conrad asked Zara. 'You can pass him the head and he can crown the snowman.'

'Of course,' she said, smiling when Conrad lifted Zach, and the boy squealed with delighted laughter.

'It's the tallest snowman ever,' the boy said, his impressed stare wide. 'Thanks, Conrad.'

When Zach rushed off to grab some fallen branches for arms, Conrad glanced over at Zara. 'Thanks for inviting me,' he said, knowing that she wouldn't have taken the decision to introduce him to Zach lightly.

'Thanks for helping,' she said, tilting her head towards the snowman. 'We couldn't have made it that tall without you. My son clearly thinks you're the coolest thing since sliced bread.'

Conrad smiled, a lump in his chest. For an unguarded second, he could so easily imagine himself a part of this little family. He hoped he and Zara would keep in touch when he returned to Australia. Perhaps she'd even visit him there, given it was on her list. But whether they stayed friends or not, the day he'd built his first snowman with her and Zach would be one he'd always remember.

CHAPTER TEN

LATER THAT EVENING, Zara sipped her wine, a shudder of contentment passing through her like an electric current, bringing her to life. The surprise day off had been magical. After the snowman, she'd invited Conrad to join her and Zach for lunch—cheese on toast and soup—then an afternoon movie, followed by board games and pasta for dinner.

In the armchair by the fire, Conrad read Zach his favourite bedtime story. Her son was totally smitten by the lodger, who'd shown him some of Australia's native animals and taught him how to say, *G'day, mate.* When Conrad had once more lifted Zach onto his shoulders to crown the head of the snowman with an old bobble hat belonging to Zara's dad, she'd wanted to cry at the look of uninhibited joy on her son's face.

Now that all the excitement of the day had died down, icy fingers of doubt once more crept down her spine. She was taking a big risk with Conrad, blurring the boundaries she'd previously never needed to enforce because she'd always kept men at arm's length and away from Zach. Today, the snow had somehow helped her to justify her out-of-character behaviour. She kept telling herself that Conrad was different. Temporary. Risk-free. But the day had left her both happy and unsettled.

Maybe because, for a blinding second, as they'd played together in the snow, she'd imagined the three of them were a family. Conrad would clearly be an amazing male role model.

'Right, time for bed, young man,' she said after Conrad finished the story and closed the book. Her boy looked exhausted from the day's excitement, and it would be business as usual tomorrow for them both—Zach back to school and Zara to work.

Zach dutifully hopped off the chair. 'G'day, mate,' he said to Conrad, offering him a final fist bump—another wonderfully exotic thing Conrad had taught him—before he dashed off to clean his teeth.

With her stomach churning with both fear and longing, Zara tucked Zach in, kissed him goodnight, and rejoined Conrad, who was picking up plastic blocks and jigsaw pieces from the floor.

'Thanks,' she said, taking a seat on the sofa. 'You don't have to do that.'

He tossed the blocks into the box. 'Thanks for

including me in your day.' He grabbed her hand and raised it to his lips, placing a brief kiss there, his stare intense. 'I know how wonderfully protective you are of Zach. I'll always remember building my first snowman with you two.'

Because Zara wanted to hurl herself into his arms and couldn't, she reached for her wine and took a massive gulp.

'I should go,' he said, hesitantly.

Zara shook her head. She should let him go, but that other side of her, the woman, not the mum, craved a little more of his company. 'Stay for a while,' she urged, patting the sofa beside her and topping up both their glasses. 'Finish your wine.'

'Okay.' Conrad folded himself onto the sofa and stretched his arm along the back.

'Zach's completely exhausted,' Zara said, desire and gratitude making her sigh. 'We don't usually pack that much excitement into one day—snow and an exotic new friend, teaching him Australian words and cool fist bumps. Thank you.' Her throat ached anew with fear that Zach was missing out on a positive male influence. Suddenly, she felt jealous of James on Zach's behalf. The poor boy had lost his father, but he still had an amazing uncle, whereas Zara was an only child.

Conrad smiled indulgently, his stare shifting

from her mouth to her eyes and turning intense in that way he had of making her feel seen. 'He's a great kid. I don't know if anyone has told you lately, but you're an incredible mum.'

'Thanks for saying that.' Zara swallowed the lump in her throat and looked away. 'It's a good job you'll be leaving soon,' she added with a teasing smile. 'A normally frazzled working mother could get used to those kinds of compliments.' And after the lovely day they'd spent together, after seeing how good Conrad was with Zach, she desperately needed the reminder that this sexy Australian with a big heart wasn't going to be around for ever.

In the beginning the temporary nature of their fling had been a huge part of his appeal. But after today, she couldn't help but wonder what might have been if he lived in the UK. A dangerous thought.

'You shouldn't doubt yourself,' he said with a frown, his fingers slowly stroking the nape of her neck in a way that turned her on.

'Sometimes, it's hard not to,' Zara admitted with a shrug that was part shudder from his touch. 'I think all parents worry that they're doing a good enough job. Parenting is the hardest thing I've ever done. Sometimes, I worry that I've ruined Zach's life by choosing the wrong man to have a baby with. I'm dreading the day he blames me because he doesn't have a father like the other kids.'

Would her boy one day resent her for her mistake? She'd always told him that his father lived in a different country, insisting she could take care of Zach as much as a mum *and* a dad combined. But those vague explanations wouldn't cut it for ever. Zach was a smart kid.

'That day may never come.' Conrad took her hand in his. 'It's like you said—you see to it that he has everything he needs. I hope my brother's wife does half as good a job with James. Man, I wish he'd been here today. He would have loved the snow and loved Zach.'

She met his stare, her pulse flying from his words and the way he looked at her, as if she was something special. Or maybe she was just seeing things because Conrad was addictive, their fling the most fun she'd had in years. But just because it had started out as nothing serious, didn't mean it wasn't…intense.

'You really love James, don't you?' she said, recalling the way he'd been protective of Zach earlier, understandable after what had happened to his brother.

'I do, of course.' He stilled, growing pensive. 'Kids have that way of making you love them.'

She understood the highs and lows of how it felt to love a child. The moments of sheer joy interspersed with the concerns that your parenting might not be up to scratch.

'You're right, they do.' She nodded, choked, because Conrad would be a wonderful father, the kind that Zach deserved. Whoa…that was an unrealistic leap.

'I was thinking about all the days, all the milestones and celebrations that my brother will miss.' His expression darkened with pain and Zara squeezed his fingers to silently let him know she was there for support.

'When Marcus made me promise that I would always look out for James after he was born, neither of us imagined that Marcus wouldn't be around to fill that role himself.' He glanced at their clasped hands, his fingers restless against hers so she guessed there was more he wanted to say, more he was feeling.

'Of course not.' Zara understood grief, and how it could come from nowhere when you least expected it. 'Are you worried about fulfilling your promise?' Since his brother died, Conrad had clearly become a more prominent male role model in his nephew's life.

'I guess.' Conrad looked up as if she'd hit the nail on the head. 'My relationship with Tessa is…complex.'

'Why?' she asked, her pulse buzzing in her fingertips with anticipation.

He watched her for a second then seemed to come to some sort of internal decision. He held her stare, doubt shifting across his expression. 'Because we used to date.'

Zara frowned, his words jarring. 'You and your sister-in-law?' That was the last thing she'd expected him to say.

'Yes.' He nodded, winced, glanced away.

Stunned, Zara fought the jealous twisting of her stomach. 'Tessa is the woman you loved? The one who broke your heart?' The one who'd left him because he'd come on too strong, too soon? Only she'd left him and turned to his brother, of all people. How confusing for Conrad.

'We'd split up long before she got together with Marcus,' he said, sounding defensive, as if he was trying to minimise how he felt about the situation. 'But as you can imagine, there's always been this kind of tension between the three of us. And it's only worsened since Marcus was killed.'

'Of course, it would be…awkward,' she said, still reeling and struggling to find the right words. Instinct told her that, for Conrad, *tension* was an over-simplification, but she could understand why he'd focussed on casual relationships since. There must be a part of him that had felt betrayed.

'Were you over her when they got together?' she asked, a hot ball of envy lodging in her chest.

Was he still in love with this woman? After all, this Tessa was the reason he didn't date.

'I was. I hadn't seen her in months. Then one day, Marcus invited me out for a beer and told me that he and Tessa had hooked up one night after running into one another at a bar. They'd been seeing each other in secret, behind my back, and Tessa was pregnant.'

Zara hid her shocked gasp. No wonder he hated secrets. No wonder he'd needed space and distance in order to properly grieve for his brother.

'How did it make you feel?' she asked, her throat aching for Conrad, who must have felt humiliated and confused and horribly torn.

He laughed, the sound mirthless, not quite meeting her gaze. 'How I felt about it didn't really matter. By the time he'd confessed it was a *fait accompli*. Tessa was having Marcus's baby, and he was going to marry her. I had the sense he'd only told me then because he knew he'd have to come clean soon, before she started showing.'

'I'm sorry,' she whispered. 'That must have been so hard on you.' Watching Marcus date Tessa, knowing that they'd gone behind his back, feeling as if he *had* to be okay with the arrangement.

His head snapped up as if she was the first to acknowledge his feelings in this complex triangle. 'I was shocked, obviously. Marcus and I were close until then. I trusted my brother more than anyone else.'

'Of course you did.' And that brotherly bond would have made the betrayal worse for Conrad. Zara waited, stroking his hand. He was downplaying it, maybe because he'd been forced to accept it.

'I didn't want to make a big deal of it,' he went on, 'or make them feel bad because they'd fallen in love. I had no lingering feelings for Tessa, so why shouldn't the two of them be happy together, especially as they were going to be parents?'

'Feelings aren't as straightforward as that,' she said. 'Your trust had been damaged. And there's an unwritten rule about exes. There must have been a part of you that felt let down. Confused. Maybe even trapped in a situation out of your control.'

No wonder he'd stopped dating seriously.

Conrad kept his gaze downcast so she knew she was close to the mark. 'I didn't want to cause a family rift or put my parents in the awkward position of having to choose a side, choose a son. They were understandably excited about the birth of their first grandchild, as they had every right to be. And then there was a wedding to plan. Everyone else just accepted it and moved on.'

'So you felt you had to do the same. As if *your* feelings, *your* hurt and betrayal didn't matter.' Zara's heart clenched painfully. He'd swallowed down his feelings for the sake of family harmony and because he loved his brother, but he obviously hadn't fully reconciled those feelings.

He shrugged, evasive. 'With time to get used to the idea, I moved on.' His mouth twitched into an approximation of a smile but it didn't reach his eyes. 'I was genuinely happy for them when they got married and James was born. They were obviously in love, and James, like Zach, is a great kid.'

Zara nodded, choked by longing. He was so kind and honourable and dependable. And he'd been forced into unhealthy coping mechanisms—setting his feelings aside, keeping his relationships casual—by circumstances brought about by the actions of others.

'Did you ever talk about it with Marcus? Tell him how you'd felt betrayed that they'd sneaked around behind your back?' she asked, hoping that, for Conrad's sake, they'd resolved it before Marcus died.

He lifted one shoulder. 'We skirted the issue a few times. I think he knew how I felt on some level. He always seemed a little guilty whenever he looked at me after that. But then life moved on. He became a husband and a father. It seemed pointless to drag up the past.'

Only now, she saw how Conrad seemed stuck in that same past.

'I'm in no way minimising your feelings, or excusing what Marcus did,' she said, 'but he must have felt guilty for hurting you and torn between his feelings for you, the brother he loved, and those for Tessa. People say we can't help who we fall in love with.'

Or was that a myth? Marcus and Tessa hadn't been forced to act on their attraction.

'I agree,' he said, meeting her stare so she saw the pain and vulnerability he hid with his 'out for a good time' persona. 'Although there must have been a moment, early on, when they both consciously crossed that line. They both chose to ignore my feelings, to sneak around. But it was Marcus that I trusted.'

And Marcus had let him down and then died.

'So it never really got resolved?' she asked, her heart breaking for the wasted opportunity. For Conrad's damaged trust and bottled-up emotions and how they held him back, even now, years later.

He shook his head, his shoulders slumped with regret. 'No. We patched over it, but it was always there like a festering wound between Marcus and me or whenever the three of us were together.

I guess a part of me figured that, one day, we'd resolve it, but now it's too late. Marcus is gone. I had to bury all the things I hadn't said to him the day we buried my brother.'

'I'm so sorry.' Zara wrapped her arm around his shoulders and held him close, their hearts banging together. 'But he would want you to be happy, just like he wanted you to be a part of his son's life, because he loved you. You can still say the things you wished you had. You can talk to him and let go of the past. It's never too late to forgive him.'

'I have forgiven him.' He pulled back and peered at her, his stare full of sadness. 'No point holding a grudge with a dead man.'

Zara nodded, uncertain if that was really true. She hoped so, for Conrad's sake. She didn't want to push him, but she was wired to care. She couldn't help but wonder if, on some level, he was stuck in the past, trying to untangle the threads of his mistrust and betrayal from his grief. He'd run away from the mess, after all.

As if he wanted to draw a line under his confession, he leaned in and pressed his lips to hers. He cupped her face, and she shuddered, relaxed her body against his and kissed him back.

'Thanks for listening to me vent,' he said when they paused for breath. But the vulnerability was gone from his stare, replaced by the desire she'd

grown used to seeing whenever they kissed. 'You
are a very special woman, Zara Wood.'

'Thanks for confiding in me,' she said, touched
that he'd trusted her enough to open up.

But no matter how close she felt to him, no
matter how much she trusted him, otherwise
she'd never have introduced him to Zach, she
had no right to try and fix him. This wasn't a relationship, just sex. And she had her own problems to work through. It was one thing to embark
on a temporary fling with a sexy colleague who
was passing through town, a whole other scenario when it came to dating someone seriously.
Finding a man she could, not only trust with *her*
feelings, but also risk making a permanent fix-
ture in her son's life, would be no easy task. That
was why she'd put it off for so long.

'I think Zach must be asleep by now,' she
whispered. 'Do you want to stay a bit longer?'
She needed to remember they were just having
a good time. No matter how wonderful Conrad
was with Zach, no matter how much she craved
both his company and his touch, no matter how
much she might wish he were sticking around,
this was still nothing serious. It couldn't be.

'I'd love to.' He cupped her cheek and smiled,
the flare of heat in his eyes telling her that, for
now, they seemed to be addicted to each other.

Time was running out. They'd be foolish not to snatch every opportunity to satiate that hunger.

Trembling inside after such an emotional day, she stood and drew him to his feet, leading him silently to her bedroom. With every footstep, she reiterated how this was temporary. Conrad would soon be heading home to the other side of the world, to his loved ones and a consultant job. She couldn't become sidetracked by his confusion and fears and trust issues. She should simply focus on this sexual journey that had begun just for fun.

She didn't want to have regrets, but nor did she want to be hurt. And if she wasn't careful, she'd confuse the professional respect and sexual connection they shared with feelings. This fling had never been about feelings, because they both had trust issues. She understood that clearly, now more than ever before.

CHAPTER ELEVEN

As HE MOVED inside Zara, Conrad's heart thudded so hard he was certain she'd feel it and understand he was caught at the centre of an emotional storm. The minute he'd opened up to her about Marcus and let her close, he'd wanted to bury himself inside her and chase away his demons and doubts with pleasure. And after such a fantastic and unexpected day spent together, part of him wanted the night to last for ever. But their chat, the way she'd effortlessly seen things he'd been reluctant to admit, perhaps even to himself, had left him feeling raw and exposed. How had she understood that being betrayed by the one person he'd trusted most in the world, his brother, had left him questioning exactly who he could ever possibly trust?

'Why is this so good?' she whispered, wrapping her legs around his hips, crossing her ankles in the small of his back, staring up at him with desire and faith as if they'd forged a new stronger bond because of their shared trust issues.

The minute they'd touched, slowly and silently stripping each other in the dim light of the bedside lamp, Conrad's urgency had turned into fierce longing he couldn't explain. He felt so close to her, he knew he would never forget his time in England. But he couldn't pretend that the relationship that had begun for fun was still under his control.

Now, with his stare locked with hers and their fingers entwined, he couldn't seem to get close enough to Zara. He couldn't breathe. Couldn't bring himself to think about the ticking clock or the time, in the not too distant future, when this would end.

'Because you're so sexy,' he said as he unhurriedly rocked his hips, refusing to think beyond the here and now. It was good because it was casual and temporary. But if he was honest, the full picture was far more nuanced. And terrifying.

Their connection was rare. She maybe didn't know it because she'd avoided casual sex since her Spanish fling, but *he* knew. It had been many years since he'd felt so in sync with a woman. Around her, his problems seemed smaller. Losing himself in their passion chased his doubts and regrets from his mind. Spending time with her, both in and out of work, put other areas of his life into sharper perspective and made him feel as if anything were possible.

'Or maybe it's because you make everything fun, even sex.' She smiled up at him and then moaned when he captured the other nipple in his mouth. 'Part of me wasn't living before you, before this.'

He groaned, moved by her admission. He'd always known that this was temporary. He would soon be heading home. He couldn't get used to the way one glimpse of Zara, one smile, brightened his day, because he'd have to leave her behind. But right then, in that moment, maybe because he'd opened up to her about Marcus's confusing disloyalty, he couldn't imagine walking away without feeling…regret. As if some part of him had been merely surviving before Zara.

'Conrad,' she moaned, wrapping her arms around his shoulders, bringing his lips back to hers, sliding her tongue into his mouth so he forgot everything but how she made him feel physically. He drove them higher and higher, moving faster and faster, nearing the point of no return, a place where he could ignore how she seemed to have changed him, the way she saw straight through him.

Her orgasm crested with a cry. He reared back, watching her fall apart, her pleasure snapping his restraint so he followed her with a groan, holding onto her tightly until the body-racking spasms died away, leaving them both spent. Panting hard, Conrad buried his face against the side of her neck and breathed in the scent of her hair, still yet to come back down from the incredible high, more aware than ever of how different this seemed. No longer just sex.

What was she doing to him? How could every time they slept together be better than the last and somehow more meaningful than any experience he'd had in years? Because he trusted *her*. That was why he'd shown her the broken version of himself tonight. He hadn't let anyone that close in a long time. But for Zara, maybe because they'd learned to trust each other at work or because she'd introduced him to her son today, or because he was leaving anyway, he'd felt safe to finally open up.

'Are you okay?' she whispered, skimming her fingers up and down his back.

'Hmm,' he mumbled, trying not to freak out as he withdrew from her body. He was far from just *okay*. He was both rejuvenated and confused. Euphoric and scared. As if, in letting her so close, some crucial part of him would never be the same. 'I've just never told anyone else what I told you earlier...' Conrad rolled onto his back.

Zara propped herself up on one elbow and watched him with a concerned frown. 'If you ever need to talk, I'm here. And I want you to know that your feelings *do* matter.'

'Thank you,' he said, too conflicted and choked to say more or even to look at her. She was too wonderful, a great listener who really cared about people. She saw him far too clearly, and part of him was desperate to keep this light and fun, nothing serious, the way it had begun.

'I know he hurt you,' she said, touching his arm. 'But I don't think your brother would want you to be emotionally stranded.'

'You never met him,' he said, even though he knew she was right. Sometimes, alone with his endlessly looping thoughts, he felt stymied. Marcus was gone. It was too late to tell him how he'd felt disregarded six years ago, but nor could Conrad seem to move on from the fact that he'd been deceived by the one person in the world he'd thought he could trust. But he wasn't ready to hear what Marcus might think or say.

'I know.' Her frown deepened with hurt. 'But he obviously loved you. I don't need to have met him to know that he wouldn't want you to be alone for ever because he'd damaged your trust in people.'

'I'll get over it,' he said, scrubbing a hand over his face and then sitting up.

'What would you say to him now, if you could?' Zara pushed, her hand on his back.

Conrad closed his eyes, part of him regretting that Zara understood him so well because he'd lowered his guard. 'I don't know.' But he'd imagined versions of the conversation a hundred times.

'I think if he hadn't been killed, you two would have worked through your issues in time. I think your relationship would have healed, because you're brothers who loved each other. I think when he asked you to be there for James, he was showing you how sorry he was and how much he respected you.'

'Maybe you're right,' he said, his throat choked and his skin crawling, because she was forcing him to examine the mess more closely. 'I'd like to be able to remember all the good times we shared and not just the one time he let me down.'

Maybe he did have unresolved feelings of betrayal that were stopping him from grieving properly. Maybe that was why he'd acted so over-protective of James. He'd never had the chance to make things right with Marcus. He didn't want to risk that he might have regrets when it came to his nephew. Maybe Zara was right: it was time to talk to his brother as if he were in the room and say all the things he'd wanted to say.

'I should go, let you get some sleep,' he said, standing. Padding to the bathroom, he tried to pull himself together in private. What was this woman doing to him, peeling away his layers like that? Yes, he felt as if he could tell Zara anything, and *he'd* been the one who'd chosen to open up, but they weren't in a proper relationship. Neither of them wanted that and even if they changed their minds, it was a dead end. She lived here and he came from the other side of the world. It would clearly take a lot for Zara to overcome her own trust issues and allow a man into Zach's life. This *had* to be temporary. He *had* to go home and sort out the mess he'd left behind. He couldn't make Zara any promises or rely on her emotional support while he tried to grieve for his brother.

He returned a little more composed, pulling on his jeans and sweater, the act of dressing like donning a much-needed suit of armour.

'I'm on the early shift tomorrow,' she said, her expression still hurt as she climbed from the bed, covering her nakedness with a fluffy dressing gown. 'I might see you on the ward.'

Guilt lashed him. She'd opened her home and her family to him today and he'd repaid her by spilling his guts and then shutting down. But she'd made him see that he'd never actually processed that damaged trust he'd felt, and now it was all tangled up with his grief over Marcus, the issue resurfacing. How was he supposed to work through all of that with Marcus gone?

'I have a ward round tomorrow,' he said, scared that by confiding in Zara, something that had come so naturally at the time, he'd failed to keep her at arm's length. But if he'd let her in, that was *his* problem, not hers. He gripped her shoulders and brushed a kiss over her lips. 'Thanks for today. I'm so honoured that you introduced me to Zach. He's a wonderful boy. You should be very proud.'

She nodded, her eyes shining with emotion as she blinked. 'You're welcome. Thanks for helping out with the snowman.'

Because he sensed she wanted to say more and he needed to collect his thoughts after such an emotional day, he moved towards the bedroom door.

'Conrad,' she said, stalling him, her breathing fast and her stare searching. 'Will you be okay?'

Conrad pressed his lips together, the urge to rush back to her and hold her in his arms until he felt his usual self almost overwhelming. Instead, he gritted his teeth, offered her his best approximation of a smile and nodded. 'See you tomorrow.'

Whatever the hell was going on inside him, whatever it was that explained his restlessness, he needed to pull it together away from Zara.

Because the way she looked at him, as if she understood him and cared about his feelings, was seriously messing with his head.

CHAPTER TWELVE

THE FOLLOWING DAY, while trying to put his feelings from the night before behind him, Conrad was halfway through his ward round on the postnatal ward when he became aware of a raised male voice. He looked up in alarm, spying Zara at the other end of the ward. Some man, obviously someone's relative, was yelling at her, his face puce with anger.

With a surge of adrenaline, all of Conrad's protective instincts fired at once. He abandoned his ward round and marched in their direction.

'I don't care if it's normal,' the belligerent relative said to Zara as Conrad approached. 'It's your job to do something.' He pointed a meaty finger, aggressively. 'My wife is very upset.'

'I understand that, sir,' Zara said, casting Conrad a quick glance before standing her ground against the hulk of a man. 'But baby blues are very common, especially after a difficult delivery like the one your wife has been through.'

The man gritted his teeth in frustration and

Conrad fought the urge to put his body between Zara and this angry guy. 'What's the problem here?' he asked, coming to Zara's defence whether she needed him or not because, just as she cared about him, he cared about *her*.

'No problem, Dr Reed,' Zara said, flicking him an impatient stare. 'I was just explaining to Mr Hancock that post-partum distress and sadness is a perfectly normal hormonal reaction to giving birth.' She kept her voice impressively calm as she addressed the man, whereas Conrad was in full-on fight-or-flight mode, and Mr Hancock was one infraction away from being marched off the ward.

'The best way to help your wife,' Zara explained soothingly, as if Conrad weren't there, 'is with plenty of reassurance and affection. The crying will pass.'

How could she be so calm, when he was genuinely scared for her safety? He couldn't stop himself from butting in. 'We don't need raised voices,' Conrad said pointedly to Mr Hancock. 'This is a maternity ward. Your wife isn't the only woman here who's just had a baby. Your outburst might be upsetting other patients. If you can't moderate your tone, you might want to go outside for some fresh air.'

'Thank you, Dr Reed,' Zara said impatiently. 'I've got this.' She had that same pitying look on her face that she'd given him as he'd left her place the night before.

Conrad baulked, feeling as if he were unravelling. He wished he could bite his tongue and not interfere. It was obvious Zara didn't need or want his help. She was an experienced midwife who valued her independence. But he couldn't help but feel protective. She was half this guy's size. If things turned physical, she could be seriously hurt.

'If you or your wife have specific concerns about the care she's receiving,' Zara went on calmly when the man stubbornly stood his ground, 'we can talk those through. Dr Reed is doing his ward round at the moment, so he'll soon be in to review your wife, but, as I said, the best medicine is love and reassurance.'

Finally, to Conrad's relief, the man ducked his head, looking sheepish. 'I'm sorry,' he said to Zara, his colour high. 'I've just never seen my wife that upset. I…don't know how to help.'

Unlike Conrad, who was slow to forgive such an unwarranted attack, Zara softened, her head tilted in sympathy. 'Why don't you make her a cup of tea?' she suggested, indicating the ward kitchen a few doors away.

Mr Hancock nodded, his body deflating. 'A cup of tea…good idea,' he said and shuffled off towards the kitchen.

Conrad stared after him, his fear still a metallic taste in his mouth. He was half tempted to drag Mr Hancock back and make him apologise to Zara again. In fact, the way he was feeling nothing short of a formal written apology would do.

'Can we have a quick word?' Zara said, her mouth tight with annoyance. She headed for the office, knowing he'd follow.

'I know I shouldn't have interrupted that second time,' he said, closing the door behind them and wishing he could drag her into his arms until he was able to breathe easy once more. 'But I just didn't care for the way he was talking to you.'

Zara watched him for a few seconds, a small frown tugging down her mouth. 'Maybe you should have allowed me to handle it from the start,' she replied, her voice clipped with frustration. 'I had the situation under control. In fact, I think your presence made him worse. I think you overreacted, Conrad.'

'Overreacted?' He gaped, his heart rate still thundering away. 'Did you see the size of that guy? He seemed angry enough to get physical.'

'He wouldn't have laid a finger on me,' Zara said, with a dismissive shake of her head and a lengthy sigh. 'He was just upset because his wife has been crying non-stop since her emergency C-section, that's all. Some men, often the big gruff ones actually, hate feeling out of control. They don't know what to do with themselves.'

'I'm not too fond of it myself,' Conrad muttered under his breath, because last night he'd let Zara too close and now it felt too late to claw back control. It was making him second-guess everything. 'But that's no excuse for raising his voice at you.'

Just as it had for Mr Hancock, Zara's expression softened with sympathy. 'I've experienced worse, Conrad. Look, I understand why you're overprotective, why you see risk everywhere, but I had the situation in hand. If I'd needed you, I would have called for you.'

Now it was his turn to frown. Of course she didn't need *him*. She didn't need any man. Not when she preferred to rely on herself. But was he hypersensitive to danger?

'I don't see risk everywhere,' he muttered, dismissing the idea that he cared too much. The last thing he wanted was to feel vulnerable and out of control like Mr Hancock. 'Of course I'm still trying to process such a senseless act of violence against my brother, a man who had just been doing his job, a man who, like you, had been trying to help someone. In some ways, I'll never understand what happened to him.'

She nodded, another of those pitying looks on

her face. 'Anyone would struggle to make sense of that,' she said, her voice soft with empathy.

'And just like paramedics, hospital staff get assaulted, both verbally and physically, all the time.' He couldn't help but want to shield her. He cared about her and her son. How could he not after everything they'd shared these past weeks? But maybe he *did* care too much. He'd let Zara close, opened up to her about Marcus, and now he couldn't seem to stop the tide of emotions. Whereas Zara was still coolly keeping men, including him, at a distance, the way she'd done since Zach was born.

'But I wasn't assaulted,' she said, quietly but firmly. 'I was dealing with the situation, and I know all about the risk-assessment procedures on the ward.'

Faced with her calm logic, he felt his stomach roll. He felt made of glass. Suddenly this fling felt way too serious. How had they arrived there so fast? Had he pitched it wrong again? Been too eager? Allowed her too close and rushed into something that wasn't reciprocated? He tried to breathe slower, dismissing the need to panic.

Zara sighed, looking at him the way she'd looked at Mr Hancock, with patience and empathy. 'I can't help but be concerned about you after last night. Perhaps your overprotective feelings— for James, for Zach, for me—are a symptom of your grief, Conrad. Maybe if you processed some of the betrayal over what Marcus did to you, maybe if you truly forgave him for hurting you, for going behind your back and making you feel that your feelings didn't matter, you could start to properly grieve for him. Otherwise how are you ever going to move on and trust someone enough for another serious relationship?'

Conrad stiffened. She was right about his unresolved feelings, ones he was still trying to untangle so he could return to Australia with a clear head. Did his concern come across as overprotectiveness? Tessa had accused him of the same thing, after all.

He sighed, scrubbing a hand through his hair. 'Maybe you're right, but I'm not the only one struggling to let go of the past, Zara. It seems it's okay for you to want to help me, but not the other way around.'

Had he blurred the line between them, confused sex with feelings? He'd started to trust Zara after all, not just professionally, but personally too. Why else would he have confided in her last night? Why else would he feel so off balance since?

'That's not true.' She frowned.

'Isn't it? You're so independent. It's one of your great strengths. But it's okay to let people help you. To allow people to care. That doesn't make you weak.'

'I know that,' she snapped, her eyes darting away.

'Do you? You don't always have to go it alone, you know. Or are you so busy punishing yourself for your mistake that you push people away so you don't have to trust them?' Conrad had assumed she'd started to trust *him*. Now he wasn't so sure. 'How are *you* ever going to have a real relationship if you won't let anyone close?'

They faced each other, stares locked, breathing hard, their accusations echoing around the room.

'I need to get back to work,' she said after a moment, her voice flat. 'I guess we're both still scared to trust for our own reasons. Going it alone has become a habit born of necessity for me. Trusting someone means letting them close to my precious boy, so you can understand why I'm protective.'

'Of course I can.' Conrad exhaled, feeling depressed. Where he'd started to imagine they might have a future, she still wasn't ready for a relationship. And even if she were, he was leaving anyway. He wasn't making her any promises. Not when he needed to return home, to work through his grief and patch up his strained relationship with Tessa so he could be there for James and keep his promise to his brother.

'I'm sorry that I interfered with Mr Hancock,' he said. 'I won't do it again.'

She raised her chin. 'I'm sorry that I offered unsolicited advice about Marcus. What do I know about relationships? At least you've had real ones before, even if you're no longer interested.'

Her words jarred, stabbing at his ribs. She wasn't wrong: he wasn't ready either. He and Zara were similar, both scared to be gullible, scared to trust, to open their hearts to something real. But last night as he'd lain awake for ages, trying to sleep, he'd tentatively wondered if, because of Zara, he might be ready to move on and start trusting people again. He'd imagined a scenario where he and Zara lived in the same country, where they might have a chance at a real relationship, be a real family with Zach. But now that she was still intent on going it alone… his doubts roared back to life.

'I'll let you go,' he said, his heart racing. He hated the distance, both physical and emotional, between them. 'I need to finish my ward round.'

'Maybe we can talk again after work?' she suggested, heading for the door. 'Once Zach is asleep.'

He nodded and tried to smile. Then he watched her leave.

As he strode back down the ward, he couldn't

shake the feeling of foreboding. Somehow, he and Zara had strayed from the casual good time they'd set out to enjoy. Even if they both wanted something real, they'd each spent years avoiding relationships. Even if they lived in the same country, there would be no guarantee that they could make it work.

He *did* care about her, that much was obvious. He just needed to keep a lid on the depth of his feelings. He'd been out of sync with a woman before when he'd dated Tessa. He'd rushed in and she'd held back, and when he'd confessed he'd fallen in love with her, she'd ended it then moved on to his brother. It wasn't that she hadn't wanted a serious relationship, she just hadn't wanted Conrad.

Resolved to double down and re-erect the barriers he'd let Zara slip past, he restarted his ward round. After all, he *had* to go home. His life was in Australia. He had to resolve things with Tessa and see James. And the panic that came whenever he thought about leaving the UK and leaving Zara behind? Clearly, that feeling wasn't reciprocated, so he'd need to do his best to ignore it.

CHAPTER THIRTEEN

LATER THAT NIGHT, Zara lay naked on top of Conrad, her face resting on the slowing thump of his heart. She'd invited him up after Zach had fallen asleep so they could talk after their earlier fight. But somehow, they'd barely apologised before they'd reached for each other, kissing voraciously as they'd stumbled towards the bedroom, shedding clothes. It was as if they each understood the futility of arguing, given that their time was running out. Instead, they'd communicated by touch, his regret left over every inch of her skin by his kisses and hers conveyed via their locked stares as he'd moved inside her, their passion for each other an all-consuming fire of which neither of them seemed to be in control.

Now, Conrad's fingers trailed up her back. Zara lay still in his arms as her mind raced and shivers of doubt raised goose pimples on her skin. She was in trouble, despite all her tough talk and independence. Addicted to his touch that made her feel alive, his secret smile that showed her his inner vulnerabilities, drawn to the way he cared deeply about people, including Zara.

And she cared too. How could she not when he'd been so horribly betrayed by the one person he'd thought he could always trust, his brother? When he had so much to offer but was scared to move beyond casual, scared or even unable to allow himself to be loved in case he got hurt again? It seemed like a vicious circle. She wanted him, more and more with every passing day. But since they'd been snowed in and he'd truly opened up to her, all the reasons this could never be anything but sex seemed glaringly obvious.

'You were right about me,' she whispered, needing him to know that, despite her earlier accusations and denials, he wasn't the only one struggling to let go of the past. 'I have been keeping people, well, men, away.'

She still carried doubts that she was ready for a real relationship. But since their closeness had deepened by working together, since she'd witnessed him interacting with her son, since he'd opened up to her about his ex and his brother, she'd begun to imagine that, with the right man, maybe she could trust her instincts again and open up her heart. Maybe she could risk letting another man, the right man, close to Zach.

His fingers stilled against her skin. 'I know. It's like you said, we've both had our trust damaged.'

Zara's throat burned with fear. Despite the way they touched each other, as if their sexual adventure was no longer just about having a good time but something more, Conrad was as broken as Zara. Whatever her feelings and imaginings, *he* couldn't be the right man. He didn't want a serious relationship, because he'd been betrayed. And he had another boy, James, to love and protect, far away in Australia.

'Perhaps I have been punishing myself,' she said, needing to be as brave as she'd urged Conrad to be. 'I've hid behind the need to put Zach first, when, really, I was just scared to trust my instincts, because they've steered me wrong before with Lorenzo.'

Scared to believe in feelings she'd had little use for these past six years while she'd put her own needs last to focus on motherhood. Scared to open her and Zach's life up to someone who might hurt them all over again.

His heart raced under her cheek, his body still as if he was holding his breath, waiting.

'But I'm also protecting Zach. I have to be careful who I allow close to him. I don't want him getting attached to someone who isn't going to stick around. For me to let someone close, I'd

need to be really serious about them.' By defini-
tion, she and Conrad were *nothing serious*, and
he wasn't sticking around.

'Of course,' he said, saying no more.

Recalling how he'd shut down her attempts
to talk about moving on the night before, recalling their fight earlier, she felt her doubts mul-
tiply. In spite of his feelings of protectiveness,
attraction, respect for Zara, he was obviously
struggling with that unresolved betrayal, hiding his trust issues behind casual relationships,
stuck because Marcus had died before Conrad
could properly forgive him. How could he ever
want a serious relationship again, when he'd been
forced to swallow down those feelings? When
he couldn't trust people not to let him down and
hurt him?

Cupping her chin, Conrad tilted her face up so
their eyes met. 'You are such an amazing person.'

She nodded, her vision swimming, because
meeting Conrad had given her hope for the future. Not that her future could include him. But
could she really find someone willing to love
both her and Zach? Could she risk being that
vulnerable, knowing the pain of possible rejection, knowing it could hurt her and her beloved
little boy? The alternative was to live her future
the way she'd lived the past six years, by just
surviving.

'Don't let that fear hold you back for ever,' he said. 'You can't swear off relationships at the age of twenty. You deserve to be happy, too.'

He brushed her lips with his and euphoria flooded her body, that happiness he said she deserved. She wanted to step into the picture he painted. But when she lowered her guard enough to think about dating, she always pictured Conrad—them working together, romantic dates followed by intense love-making, her, Zach and Conrad laughing together the way they had the day of the snow.

But that was crazy, naive, the kind of dream younger Zara would have entertained, and look where that had led. To heartache and loneliness. Conrad was still caught up in the past and not even thinking about relationships, and she'd always known this would be temporary and that he'd go home. She'd most likely never see him again. If she wasn't careful with her wild imaginings, if she made another mistake, allowed another man close enough to hurt her, the consequences would be bigger, because Zach was old enough to understand and remember and feel rejected.

When she pulled back from his kiss, Zara deliberately changed the subject so she could dismiss the fear that it might be too late to protect herself where he was concerned. 'What about you? What will you do when you go back to Australia? Do you have a consultant job lined up?'

'No,' he said, stiffening slightly. 'I've applied for more locum work in Brisbane.'

'Why?' she asked, confused. 'Isn't it time you became a consultant?' Conrad was an experienced senior registrar. She understood why he'd wanted to locum in England—a temporary post that had allowed him to gain some distance from his complicated relationship with Tessa, and to grieve. But more locum work in Brisbane made no sense.

'I'm just not ready,' he said, sounding defensive. 'I don't know where I want to settle.'

Zara's heart sank. If she'd needed more confirmation that he was still struggling with the past, still running away from his feelings of betrayal, this was it. If he wasn't ready to settle in Australia, he was even less likely to be thinking about relationships, whereas naive Zara was getting carried away again.

'But surely you'd stay where your family are,' she said sitting up and drawing the sheet over her body. 'Where James is? Brisbane?'

Ever since he'd told her of his and Tessa's history, she'd tried valiantly to ignore her jealous imaginings of them fixing their relationship and maybe getting back together one day. Who Conrad dated in the future, who he fell in love with, was none of Zara's business. She had no claim to him. But clearly, she was already way too emotionally invested.

'Yes, that's the plan,' he said, cagily. 'But, I don't know… I've really enjoyed my time working in the NHS. It's made me think about the kind of consultant post I want.'

Zara froze, her breath trapped in her lungs. He couldn't mean he'd considered moving to the UK, could he? She was too scared to ask. But her reaction to the idea, the elation that hijacked her pulse, spoke volumes. She was already in deep. If Conrad lived in England, if he wanted a real relationship, she'd want to continue to see him, to build on what they had and see where it could go. She would even, albeit slowly, allow him and Zach to get to know each other, because she trusted him and liked the kind of man he was.

But none of that could be.

'What about James?' she whispered, terrified and torn to shreds by her conflicted feelings. Part of her, that newly awakened part that clearly had feelings for Conrad, wanted him to stay. But she couldn't ask him to, nor could she rely on her instincts, her feelings, not when they'd steered her so wrong before.

'Yes. That's where I always end up, too,' he said, his voice quiet and thoughtful. 'I owe it to my brother to make sure James is okay, to patch up things with Tessa so I can be the uncle he needs. So I'll go back to Brisbane, and just…see how things pan out, I guess.'

Zara's dangerous excitement drained away, leaving chills behind. How stupid was she to get her hopes up like that? Had she learned nothing from Lorenzo's rejection? No amount of waiting patiently or staring at the phone would make it ring, just as no amount of naive wishing would make someone care when they didn't, or *couldn't* because they'd been hurt before too.

'Speaking of James,' he said, 'I wanted to ask you something.'

Her pulse accelerated again, but this time she shut down the foolish hope.

'There's a steam train exhibition at the weekend I thought Zach might like,' he said, his stare full of boyish excitement the way it had been the day they'd built a snowman. 'I'm on call Saturday, but we could go Sunday. You can ride on the train, and they serve high tea on board. We could make a day of it.'

Zara swallowed, her head all over the place, knowing she'd have to decline. It sounded innocent enough, and, like James, Zach loved trains. But exposing her son to any more of Conrad when he was already pretty smitten with 'the Aussie lodger' and when Conrad was leaving soon was too risky. If she spent another day with Conrad, watching him interact wonderfully with Zach again, she'd never be able to keep her volatile feelings in check. She couldn't let him any closer. If she did, she might not survive him leaving.

'Um…can I think about it?' she said, her eyes stinging. 'I usually catch up on housework and laundry at the weekend,' she finished lamely. But there was no point wishing for the impossible. She'd learned that the hard way while waiting for Zach's father to have a change of heart and seek a relationship with his son.

'Of course,' he said, his voice flat, pricking at her guilt.

This time it was Zara who got up from the bed first and locked herself in the bathroom. She faced her reflection, resolved to protect herself better, given their time was running out and Conrad would soon be gone. The only sure-fire way to safeguard her emotions as resolutely as she protected Zach was to end this now. To stop sleeping with him and part as friends.

She glanced at the closed door, her heart banging away painfully under her ribs as she imagined him on the other side—sexy, confused by her caginess, emotionally vulnerable because he was as susceptible to rejection as Zara. She couldn't imagine she possessed the strength to work with him and not want him with the same burning ferocity she'd always felt. Maybe she could hold on for one more week. Lock down her confusing feelings, take as much of him physically as she could get in the time they had left and face the emotional consequences when he stepped on the plane.

CHAPTER FOURTEEN

LATER THAT WEEK, Conrad was on his way to the delivery ward after a morning of surgeries, when he received an urgent call from his SHO, Max. He rushed to the ward, his adrenaline pumping. When he entered the delivery suite, Zara, Sharon and Max were with the patient, an anaesthetist and paediatrician standing by in the corner of the room.

'What's the situation?' Conrad asked, meeting Zara's concerned stare as he quickly pulled on some gloves.

'Shoulder dystocia,' Zara said, valiantly keeping the alarm he saw in her eyes from her voice. 'The baby's head was delivered three minutes ago. Mum's name is Gail.'

Zara appeared understandably panicked as the labouring woman gave a moan to signal another contraction. But there was no time to comfort either of them. Shoulder dystocia, a serious birth complication with consequences for the health of the mother and baby, meant the baby's shoulders were trapped in the mother's pelvis, delaying the birth of the body.

Conrad took the position beside Zara in place of his SHO, too focussed on the emergency to wonder why Zara had called Max and not him. He quickly examined the patient, glancing at the foetal heart rate monitor for signs that the baby was in distress.

'Okay,' he said, taking charge. 'Let's try the McRoberts manoeuvre. Zara, you take the right leg, Max the left. Gail, the baby is a little stuck. We need to shift your position to help deliver the shoulders.'

As another contraction began and at Conrad's nod, his assistants flexed the patient's hips, bringing her knees up towards her armpits while Conrad placed his hand on her lower abdomen and applied pressure to the front of the pelvis. 'Push now, as hard as you can,' he instructed the patient.

With everyone present seemingly holding their breath, willing the situation to resolve, the baby moved slightly, but then retreated back into the birth canal.

As Gail collapsed back onto the pillow, clearly exhausted, Conrad looked up and made eye contact with a worried-looking Zara. A week ago he'd have seen respect and faith and encouragement in her stare, but now he just saw doubt. He wanted to reassure her that, together, they could safely deliver this baby, to ask her to believe in him, but even if there was time, even if they'd been alone, he was no longer as sure of Zara. Things had changed between them, as if they were both protecting themselves for the inevitable end of their fling, which was, of course, eminently sensible.

'One more push now,' Conrad said as the next contraction started. 'We're nearly there.' They performed the manoeuvre again, and this time, the shoulders were successfully delivered to a collective sigh of relief around the room.

Conrad completed the delivery of the newborn, placing the baby onto Gail's stomach before he quickly clamped and cut the cord and noted the baby's Apgar score.

'Well done, Gail,' he said. 'He seems fine, but the paediatrician will give him a quick check over, okay? Then he's all yours. Congratulations.'

He glanced up at Zara, yearning for that closeness he'd grown accustomed to whenever they worked together, but Zara seemed distracted. He couldn't help but recall how she'd withdrawn from him the other night when he'd suggested an outing with Zach. He understood that she was choosing to protect her son, and maybe herself, too. And he couldn't blame her. After all, he was making her no promises. In fact, ever since their fight, he too was desperately trying to protect himself.

But ever since the snowman, since the night he'd told her about Marcus and Tessa, he'd also started to imagine a different future for them, one where, instead of ending their fling when he left for Australia, he returned to England and they picked up where they'd left off. Dated for real. A serious relationship. But just because he was trying to manage his own confusion and doubts by selfishly blurring the lines, didn't mean Zara owed him anything. She'd admitted to always relying on herself, and he could understand why, given how she'd been hurt.

Despite the crazy ideas spinning in his head, the ways they could continue to see each other, he repeatedly came up against the same brick wall: Zara wasn't ready to take that risk for a relationship. If Conrad allowed her any closer or pushed for some grand gesture where one of them shifted their entire life to the other's country, he might discover that it was *him* she didn't want. Better to keep any promises off the table, to fly to Australia next week as planned and sort out his personal life. Maybe then his head would clear and he could think straight.

With all the excitement over and with his stomach still twisting with doubt, Conrad washed up and headed for the office to make a note in the patient's file. That complete, he went in search of Zara, finding her in the ward kitchen.

'What happened?' he asked, trying and failing to keep the accusation from his voice. 'Why didn't you call *me*?'

She looked up at him and sighed, her fatigue obvious. 'It all happened so quickly. Everything was progressing normally until it suddenly wasn't. Max was already on the ward.'

She ducked her stare from his and busied herself making toast. Reluctant to cause another argument, Conrad bit his tongue. He wasn't doubting her story, but there was something off with her. She couldn't look at him. A sickening sense of déjà vu took him back to that first week, when they hadn't really known each other at all. When she'd been prickly, keeping him at arm's length, locking down any need for feelings as she'd done since she'd been hurt by that last guy.

Conrad sighed, terrified that the intense feelings he couldn't seem to contain, ones that fuelled those fantasies of uprooting his life and moving to the UK on the off chance that Zara might be interested, were his alone. He'd rushed into things before, with Tessa. From the way Zara seemed to be pulling back, reluctant to expose Zach to Conrad, reducing her professional reliance on him, Zara was obviously still happy to go it alone.

'Are you okay?' he asked, concerned because obstetric emergencies took their toll on everyone concerned and shoulder dystocia, which was fortunately relatively rare, could alarm the most experienced midwife.

'I'm fine,' she said, finally looking his way. 'It's been a long shift, that's all. I'm tired.'

He was just about to reach out and touch her, the urge automatic, when Sharon bustled into the kitchen. The older midwife paused, shooting Conrad a peculiar look before she moved to the sink and filled a water jug.

'How are you, Sharon?' Conrad asked. 'That was a bit of a shock for us all, I think.'

'I'm glad for the outcome,' Sharon said, catching Zara's eye before she looked Conrad's way. 'A great team effort.'

While Zara finished making the toast, Sharon discreetly made her exit, but something in the older woman's manner flushed his body with uncomfortable heat. The hairs on the back of Conrad's neck stood on end. Was he being paranoid? He sensed they'd talked about him behind his back. But surely Zara wouldn't do that after everything he'd confided in her and after she'd insisted on secrecy?

When they were alone again, he lowered his voice. 'Does she know about us?' he asked, his paranoia spilling free.

Zara shook her head, looking insulted. 'I haven't told her, but she suspects I'm seeing someone.' She looked up and met his stare. 'I'm rubbish at hiding my *post-sex glow*, apparently.' She rolled her eyes, her humour returning for a second. But the smile was tinged with sadness, as if she too sensed this disconnect between them and had no energy to fix it.

As he recalled her obvious fatigue, a surge of compassion welled inside him. He knew first-hand how shift work could mess with your sleep patterns and she also had Zach to care for.

'Listen,' he said, lowering his voice. 'I know it's Friday.' He paused, knowing she would un-derstand he was speaking about their standing late-night arrangement when Zach was sleeping over at his grandmother's. 'But why don't you get an early night tonight?'

He would miss her, ache for her, but maybe he was being selfish. Maybe a bit of distance would help them both gain some perspective. After all, by next weekend this would be over and he'd be on a plane back to Australia. Then, touching her, kissing her reaching for her in the night, would be physically impossible.

She placed a steaming mug of tea on the tray and looked up. 'That's not a bad idea, actually. I could do with an early night.'

Conrad nodded, his pulse whooshing through

his head. He wanted to kiss her, to ease her burden somehow, to care for her the way she cared for everyone around her, but he wasn't her boyfriend. She didn't need or want one of those and he was leaving anyway.

'About this weekend…' Zara's mouth flattened into a frown, her stare darting away. 'I'm sorry, but I don't think it's a good idea.' She looked up, something in her expression hardening, reminding him of the woman he'd first met, a woman who'd needed no one. 'Ever since the snowman, Zach has been asking about you non-stop. You made quite the impression on him. I'm scared that if he spends any more time with you, when you're gone, he'll be sad. I don't want to make it worse for him, no matter what I want for myself. I *have* to put him first.'

Conrad nodded, his stomach sinking. 'Of course, you do. I understand. I wouldn't want him to be sad either.' Of course she was protecting Zach. Her priorities were what they'd always been. Conrad's hadn't changed either. They'd always been on this trajectory, their fling temporary. He'd just got carried away by his feelings, lured by the idea that if they lived in the same country, it could be more than temporary. And that vulnerable, irrational part of him that had let her closer than he'd let anyone in six years couldn't help but feel a moment's bitterness. He'd been useful for a sexual adventure, but could never be anything serious, not when she was still dead set on holding men away.

She nodded, picking up the tray as if the conversation was closed. 'Thanks for understanding.'

'Just out of curiosity,' he said, before she could leave, his heart leaping in his chest, 'and because I clearly like to torture myself, if I wasn't flying to Australia next week, would your answer have been any different?'

Hypothetically, had they ever stood a chance of something more than just sex?

'I don't know,' she whispered, looking down. 'But I do know that I'm always going to choose to protect Zach. I'm his mother, so it comes with the territory.' She shrugged, sadly.

Conrad nodded, unable to argue with her inevitable and admirable choice, but crushed all the same.

'I'd better take this tea to Gail, before it goes cold.' She moved past him with the tray.

'Zara,' he said, before she'd gone too far. 'I'll miss you tonight.'

'Me too,' she said, walking away anyway.

But then they both needed to get used to doing that, because time was running out.

CHAPTER FIFTEEN

LATER THAT NIGHT, Conrad's door opened and Zara rushed into his arms out of the cold. 'I tried to stay away, but I couldn't do it. I know it's only going to make it worse when you leave, but I can't seem to care. I just want you until I can't have you any more.'

She stood on tiptoes, raised her mouth to his, kissing him deeply, passionately, her heart soaring when he returned her kisses, like for like.

'Thank goodness,' he said, kicking closed the door.

Even before she heard it slam, she was tugging at his clothes. 'Hurry,' she urged, needing him with terrifying desperation. 'I need you.'

She gasped as one of his hands grasped her backside and the other cupped her breast, his lips caressing the ticklish spots on her neck. She'd spent the entire rest of the day trying to justify this rendezvous, telling herself that as long as she kept Conrad away from Zach, only *her* feelings were at risk. Telling herself she could handle the emotional danger if she focussed on the sex. Telling herself she'd deal with any fallout when he was gone, just as she'd always relied on herself.

'I was sitting here, staring at the door, willing you to change your mind.' He kissed her again, stripping off her jumper and jeans before scooping her from the floor and carrying her into the bedroom with her legs wrapped around his waist. 'I'm so glad you did.'

He tumbled them onto the bed, his hips, the hard jut of his erection, between her legs, where she wanted him. But there were still too many layers between them and not enough skin-to-skin contact.

'Conrad,' she moaned, caressing his erection through his jeans as she pushed her tongue into his mouth. When he stood to remove his clothing and reached for the bedside drawer and the stash of condoms he kept there, she shimmied off her underwear.

'Will it stop?' she asked as he joined her on the bed, pressing kisses all over her body. 'This burning need? Tell me it will stop when you go,' she begged, needing to hear that she'd go back to normal, even if it was a lie.

He looked up, confusion and lust slashed across his handsome face. 'I don't know. I hope so. For both our sakes.' Then he buried his face between her legs, kissing her deeply with a tortured groan.

Because his touch, this wild passion, were the only things that could block out the loud ticking of the clock in her head, Zara lost herself to the oblivion of pleasure. While she was focussed on the way he made her body come alive, she didn't have to think about how, but for the fact he wasn't the right man to risk her heart with, she could so easily fall for him. She'd let him close, closer than anyone else, ever, and one day soon, she had to pay the price for that recklessness. But not yet. For a few more days she could hold off the inevitable sadness that would come when he left.

When he reared back, covered himself with the condom and pushed inside her, she clung to him, all but wrecked by the force of their uncontrollable need for each other. But this had always been too good, intense, a thrilling and passionate risk. 'Yes,' she cried as he gripped her hand and moved his hips, slow and deep.

'I can't stop wanting you,' he said, his face a mask of dark desire as he raised her thigh over his hip so he sank deeper, his body scorching her every place they connected. 'I can't stop counting the days.'

'Don't,' she said, shaking her head. 'Let's just enjoy every second, no regrets.' This had started with sex. Only fitting that they should keep it about sex, until the very end.

She'd had a minor wobble there for a few days, allowed her imagination to run wild with impossible what ifs, but her head was back on straight now.

'Zara,' he groaned as their bodies moved in unison, his thrusts pushing her higher and higher towards the release she'd come for. As the rhythm of their bodies built to a crescendo, Zara focussed on the pleasure, her orgasm ripping through her in powerful waves until all she could do was hold him as he crushed her in his arms, burying his face against the side of her neck, groaning.

When his body stilled, Zara closed her eyes and breathed him in, trying to memorise his unique scent, already certain she was falling for Conrad Reed. But that was okay. She'd come to terms with it, compartmentalised it the way she'd done for so many other parts of her life since becoming a mother. When you had a child you needed to put first, your own feelings didn't really matter.

Conrad raised his face from the crook of her neck, his eyes stormy. 'Part of me wishes I could stay,' he whispered, kissing the palm of her hand, and Zara's heart clenched.

She nodded and pushed his hair back from his

face. 'Part of me wishes you didn't have to go. But we always knew it was temporary. I'll never forget my wild sexual adventure with you.'

Witnessing the doubt her words caused, she shifted under his weight. Their wishes made sense. Their relationship had always been intense, even when it was just fun. But wishes weren't reality, and when she was finally ready to fully open up her heart to a real adult relationship, she needed to be a hundred per cent certain it was with the right man, preferably one who lived in the same country. She wouldn't risk confusing Zach, nor would she expose her sweet little boy to any more rejection.

He rolled to the side and released her. Zara stood and hunted around for her scattered clothes.

'You don't want to stay?' he asked, his voice uncertain, so she winced with guilt. If only she'd possessed the stamina to resist him tonight, to start weaning herself off instead of selfishly taking every kiss and touch she could get.

'Just because I couldn't fight the temptation to be with you, I'm still tired.' Zara swallowed down the almost overwhelming urge to climb back into his warm bed and hold him all night long. 'I'll sleep better in my own bed.'

She pulled on her clothes, pressed one last kiss to his lips and hurried out into the bitterly cold night, where, finally, she was able to draw a deep breath. Only as hard as she tried to forget it, the look of confusion, doubt and hurt on his face as she'd left kept her awake for half of the night.

CHAPTER SIXTEEN

ON CONRAD'S FINAL day at Abbey Hill Hospital, Zara sat in the break room just outside the delivery suite with Sharon, feeling as if her world were about to implode. Zach had been sick all weekend with a cold, so she'd had to swap shifts with Bella. Since working three night shifts in a row, she hadn't seen Conrad since last Friday, when they'd made love as if preparing for the end of the world and then she'd fled. But with every day that passed where they didn't see each other, she felt a sick kind of triumph, as if she was already winning the battle of missing him, even before he'd left the country.

She picked at her salad, her head all over the place and her appetite non-existent. Now that the day of Conrad's departure was nearly upon them, Zara had a more pressing dilemma than fearing she might not get over the most intense relationship of her life—her late period.

'Two across,' Sharon said, breaking into Zara's reverie. 'A sudden attack. Four letters. Starts with an R.' Sharon was focussed on the crossword puzzle at the back of one of the magazines lying around the break room, as if this were just any other day. Of course, Sharon wasn't aware that Zara had slept with the sexy Australian locum, that she'd embarked on a foolish fling with him and developed deep feelings for him. That she might, if fate were cruel enough to throw not one, but two unplanned pregnancies her way, be having his baby.

'Raid,' Zara said absently, grateful to have something else to think about other than the fear burning a hole in her chest. She and Conrad had always used condoms, but they'd also had a lot of sex.

Sensing something was off with her friend, Sharon looked up from the magazine crossword. 'What's wrong? You've been off all morning.'

'I'm just tired,' Zara tried to bluff. But one look at Sharon's serious expression told her there was no point in trying to hide her concerns from the other woman. They were probably written all over Zara's face.

'I realised this morning that my period is a couple of days late, that's all,' she said with a sigh. Just saying the words sent her mind into a panic. What if she was pregnant? Would she have to raise this baby alone, too? She and Conrad weren't a couple. He was leaving tomorrow. And Australia was even further away than Spain…

But surely history wouldn't repeat itself…? Surely she couldn't have made another mistake? She swallowed, feeling queasy. How could she have been so reckless again? Yes, she'd practised safe sex and taken every possible precaution, but she should have known better than to take risks with a man who came from the other side of the world. A man who was emotionally unavailable because, like her, he was scared to rush into another relationship. A man she'd always known she couldn't have.

Sharon frowned, obviously concerned. 'Have you taken a pregnancy test?'

'I've been busy today, delivering other people's babies,' she said lamely, shaking her head and pushing away her lunch.

Part of her had wanted to stay happily in denial, hoping that if she left it long enough, her period would start and there'd be no need to wait for those pink lines to appear. No need to tell Conrad of the possibility. No need to know that it wouldn't make any difference to their readiness for a relationship. Just the possibility of a pregnancy had reopened feelings from the past—shame at her own stupidity, guilt that she might be about to mess Zach's life up even more, a resurgence of Lorenzo's cruel rejection—feelings she'd thought she'd conquered, but obviously hadn't.

'Busy having sex, by the sounds of it,' Sharon said. At Zara's sharp look, her friend turned sympathetic. 'Is your mystery man our sexy Australian locum by any chance?'

Zara gaped, her jaw slack as she ducked her head away from Sharon's expression of pity. 'How did you figure that out?'

'I have eyes,' Sharon said, closing the magazine. 'Perhaps you're too close to see it, but he looks at you with this kind of feral hunger. He seems devastated when you're not on the ward and smiles more when you're around. It's kind of obvious. We've all noticed.'

Zara blinked away the sting in her eyes, feeling stupid and naive. Could everyone she worked with also see how close she'd come to falling hard for Conrad? And now she might be having his baby…

'Yes, well, so much for "getting back out there" and "having a good time".' She threw two of Sharon's favourite arguments for why Zara should date back at her. 'Now look where I've ended up.'

Sharon tilted her head in sympathy. 'It might be negative. You won't know until you take the test.'

Zara nodded, feeling sick and imagining it was down to morning sickness. Of course, her practical friend was right. 'I'll grab one from the hospital pharmacy on my way home. Take it tonight,' Zara said, glancing at the clock, her stomach twisting as she packed away her uneaten lunch. Their break time was over.

'What if it is positive?' Sharon cautiously asked. 'I'm guessing he's still planning to leave tomorrow?'

'Of course he is. It was nothing serious. Just a sexual fling, the kind you've been telling me to have for the past six years.' Time to put to bed any naive notion that she and Conrad could possibly have a future. She had Zach to think about. Conrad had his own life to lead, grieving to do, his nephew to support.

'Unless it *is* positive,' Sharon pushed, 'which might change things...'

'It won't.' Zara shook her head, cutting Sharon off. She refused to think of that possibility. 'I'm almost certain it will be negative, and even if we wanted a relationship, which neither of us does, because we've both got trust issues, we're from different continents. We both have jobs and lives and commitments. Real life doesn't always work out.'

She swallowed, aware of the sickening similarities between her holiday fling with Lorenzo and her fling with Conrad. She'd known going into both that neither of them would last.

'Then I'll say no more.' Sharon stood, picked up her bag and eyed Zara with compassion that set Zara's teeth on edge. 'But please text me when you know the result of the test or I'll worry, too.'

'I will. And please don't tell anyone else about me and Conrad. I forced him to keep it a secret, because it was nothing serious and always temporary. I didn't want you lot teasing me, and I knew I'd never hear the last of it, having put off dating for so long.' She couldn't bring herself to say the word sex now, not when what she and Conrad had been doing felt bigger than just sex. It felt like a relationship. A *real* relationship. But of course, it wasn't.

'Of course I won't,' Sharon said, looking worried.

'And please don't look at me like that,' Zara pleaded. 'Everything is going to be fine. The test will be negative. Conrad will leave tomorrow. And life will go back to normal around here.'

As they left the break room together and headed back to the delivery ward, Zara wondered how many times she'd have to repeat the last point until she believed it.

Later that afternoon, Conrad had just finished discharging some patients with Max, when an alarm sounded outside the delivery ward. He took off running, aware of footsteps behind him.

At the lifts, a flashing light told him some sort of emergency was occurring inside. He skidded to a halt, glancing around, relieved to see that Sharon and Zara were there too.

But there was no time to talk. A second later, the lift doors opened. A couple in their twenties were inside, the man supporting his heavily pregnant partner from behind. The woman clearly in second-stage labour.

'The baby's coming. Now!' she cried in a state of panic. 'I can't walk any further.' With that, a contraction took hold and she bared down, her weight supported by her partner.

'We'll get supplies,' Sharon said, grabbing Max and running back to the delivery ward.

Conrad pulled some gloves from the pocket of his scrubs, passing Zara a pair before pulling on his own. Together, they crouched side by side in front of the woman, blocking the lift doors from closing.

'What's your name?' Zara asked.

'Jessica,' the woman panted, moaning as another contraction began.

'We can't move her.' Zara shot Conrad a look.

'I agree,' he said as Sharon and Max returned with medical supplies and extra pairs of hands. Sharon unfolded a mobile privacy screen across the opening of the lift behind Zara and Conrad, blocking the view of anyone who happened to walk past.

With the screen in place, Conrad raised the woman's dress to her waist and Zara removed her underwear and quickly examined her. 'I can feel the head,' Zara said, meeting Conrad's stare. 'She's fully dilated.'

He nodded, grateful that she was there. Her calm manner was exactly what they needed, because, whether they liked it or not, they'd be delivering this baby in the lift, any second now.

'Jessica, you need to listen to us,' Zara said, fitting the cardiotocography or CTG sensors around Jessica's abdomen to pick up the baby's heart rate. 'When we tell you to stop pushing, we need you to pant, okay?'

The woman nodded, her eyes wild with fear and pain. Conrad laid the towels and a sheet that Sharon passed to him on the floor of the lift. Jessica's moan heralded the start of the next contraction. While she pushed, crouched in front of and supported by her partner, Conrad and Zara held their hands out at the ready to catch the baby if things happened quickly.

'Okay, pant now, Jessica,' Zara instructed the patient as the baby's head emerged.

Conrad quickly loosened the umbilical cord from around the baby's neck, while Sharon passed in more clean towels. Zara had just managed to spread them over her lap, when the rest of the baby was delivered into Zara and Conrad's waiting hands.

'It's a girl, Jessica,' Conrad said with a smile of relief, noting the baby's Apgar score. He and Zara held onto the newborn who'd been so eager to arrive, smiling at each other, laughing now the adrenaline rush was over.

While the parents laughed and cried and peered in wonder at their daughter, Zara cleaned up the baby with a towel and then handed her over. Conrad injected Jessica's thigh with syntocinon to help the uterus contract down to deliver the placenta and then he clamped and cut the umbilical cord.

'We're going to move you to a delivery suite now, Jessica,' Conrad said as Sharon wheeled in a wheelchair. 'So you can deliver the placenta.'

He glanced at Zara, hoping to see the same euphoria he felt in her eyes. That they'd delivered this baby together, practically hand in hand, made him feel closer to her than ever. But to his utter alarm, she looked close to tears. She wouldn't look at him. What was going on?

In a flurry of activity, Jessica was helped into the wheelchair by Zara and her husband, while Sharon and Max collected up the equipment.

'Do you want me to help with third stage?' Conrad asked Zara, reluctant to just walk away after such an emotionally fraught delivery. He wanted to wrap his arms around Zara and kiss away her frown.

'I've got it,' she said, barely looking his way. But perhaps she was simply focussed on the patient, on completion of the third stage of labour and performing the baby's neonatal checks after such an unorthodox delivery.

As Zara whisked Jessica and her newborn to a nearby delivery suite, ward orderlies started the clean-up, wheeling in a laundry bin and removing the screens. A hospital security guard appeared to lock the lift doors open while the cleaning was carried out. Concerned about Zara, Conrad wheeled the portable oxygen cylinder they fortunately hadn't needed and followed Sharon onto the ward and into the utility room.

'Well, that was a first,' Sharon said with a chuckle, disposing of the used syringe in the sharps bin.

Conrad nodded, parking the oxygen cylinder against the wall. 'Is Zara okay? She seemed… upset.' He knew the two women were close. Perhaps Zara had confided in Sharon about him leaving tomorrow.

Sharon ducked her head guiltily as she busied herself with the clear-up, and Conrad immediately knew that she knew about their fling.

'She'll be fine…' Sharon said, busying herself

and not looking at him. 'Births can be an emotional experience, as you know, and she's probably just distracted. I told her to get a pregnancy test as soon as possible, that way she'll know for certain, although—' She broke off, finally realising that she'd maybe said too much.

Conrad froze, his blood chilling. Zara was pregnant?

Sharon turned to face him, clearly horrified that she'd let it slip. 'You didn't know, did you?' she said, her hand covering her mouth. 'I'm so sorry. I just assumed… It just slipped out. She's not certain,' she rushed on. 'In fact she's adamant it will be negative. She's going to buy a test on the way home… Perhaps she didn't want to tell you until she knew for sure.'

Conrad's stomach rolled. Not only did Sharon seem to know all about him and Zara and their fling, Zara had also confided in her friend that she might be pregnant. And yet she hadn't confided in *him*? Not even when he was the father. She obviously didn't trust him.

Sharon sagged in defeat, resting her back against the edge of the sink. 'What will you do?'

Conrad scrubbed a hand over his face, his mind racing with possibilities. 'Talk to her, of course. Make sure she's okay. I had no idea.' He'd always wanted a family of his own with the right woman, someone he loved, who loved him back and wanted him in her life…

Sharon nodded. 'I think that's a good plan. The two of you obviously have some stuff to sort out.'

Just then, Max poked his head into the room. 'There's a woman with an ectopic pregnancy in A & E.'

Conrad nodded and moved towards the door on autopilot, glancing back at Sharon. 'I have to go. Clearly it's going to be one of those crazy days.'

Sharon tilted her head, concern in her eyes. 'Want me to pass on a message to Zara?'

Conrad shook his head, feeling sick. The waiting emergency meant he had no time to think and no idea what he wanted to say to Zara anyway. 'Thanks, but I'll catch her later.'

Shelving his sense of betrayal that Zara had gone behind his back to her friend before coming to him, he hurried down the stairs to A & E with Max.

CHAPTER SEVENTEEN

THAT NIGHT, AFTER an evening spent operating on the ectopic pregnancy case, Conrad took his usual seat on Zara's sofa, his chest hollowed out with a sad sense of inevitability. So many times this past month he'd sat in this very seat, laughing with this woman, talking to her, kissing. He'd poured his heart out, told her about his brother, his grief, his shameful feelings of betrayal. Now he wasn't sure that he'd really known her at all. Because the pain he'd felt earlier at the hospital when he'd realised she'd kept a secret and gone behind his back to her friend had burned him alive. It was as if he'd never meant anything to her.

'Sharon said she'd let slip that my period was late,' Zara said, taking the seat beside him. 'I told you there was no privacy at work.'

'Is that all you care about? Secrets?' he asked, because, as far as he was concerned, an unplanned pregnancy with this woman wouldn't have been the worst thing in the world. He cared about her and her son. He trusted her. He'd assumed she'd trusted him. That they were moving in the right direction. That, but for his departure to Australia, they'd both want to continue their relationship. Before he'd found out that there might be a baby, he'd even been plotting ways he could return to the UK so he could see her again and take what had started as something casual and fun as the foundation for a real relationship.

But now, he was almost scared to find out how she felt. For some reason, maybe because he was reminded of the last time he'd cared about a woman and she too had gone behind his back, it felt that Zara was about to break up with him. But there was no need. They'd never been an item.

'Of course not,' she said, her frown turning to an encouraging smile. 'But it's okay. I'm *not* pregnant.' Her face lit up. 'I took a test when I got home from work this afternoon and it's negative.'

He met her stare, seeing nothing but relief and that distance she'd worn for the past week, whereas Conrad felt crushed. His heart, which had been pounding, plummeted to his boots. He hadn't properly had time to think about how he felt about Sharon's revelation, but with Zara's confirmation that there was no baby, all he felt was desolate disappointment.

'That's a relief,' he mumbled automatically,

picking up on Zara's feelings on the matter. No point missing something that had never been. And now he knew exactly how out of sync his feelings were with Zara's.

'Yes.' She looked down at her hands in her lap. 'So you can leave tomorrow with your mind at rest. There's no reason to feel obligated or to stay in touch.'

She was practically pushing him out of the door. Obviously Zara's feelings for him were nowhere near as strong as his for her. He'd moved too fast again. Judged it wrong. Poured out his heart to a woman who could never need or want him because she still wasn't ready to let him, or any other man, close.

'I'm sorry that you had to find out from Sharon,' she said, meeting his stare. 'I didn't intend to tell her, but she knows me so well. She knew I was worried about something.'

'You could have told *me*,' he said, hating that, for a few hours, he might have hypothetically fathered a child and been the last to know, just as he'd been the last to know when his brother had fallen for his ex. 'Especially when you knew that the last woman I cared about also went behind my back.'

'You're right,' she admitted, looking shamefaced. 'I'm sorry. But after Zach being sick all weekend and after my night shifts, I only noticed the date this morning. I didn't want to text you and there was no point worrying you if I wasn't pregnant, which as it turned out was the right call, because I'm not.' She smiled brightly then, and he shrank inside a little more.

'And more importantly, you don't need me or my emotional support, right? You never have, not when you can go it alone, same as always.'

She was so terrified of trusting the wrong guy, and she clearly didn't trust *him*. Whereas he'd been looking for more locum work nearby, taking Sharon's advice and wondering if there'd soon be a consultant job available in Derby and wondering how quickly he could return to the UK.

'That's not fair,' she said with a frown. 'I didn't set out to tell Sharon first, but she *is* my friend. And I didn't tell her that we've been having sex. She'd already figured it out by herself.'

Conrad nodded, glancing away, his doubts so acute, he wondered if he was once more over-reacting. It wouldn't surprise him. His feelings were out of control, after all. One minute he was convinced he had to leave as planned, the next he was plotting ways to stay.

'So that's all I am to you still? Just sex?' he asked, the panicked thudding of his heart inten-sifying. He and Zara could only work if they were on the same wavelength. For over a week, he'd tentatively tried and failed to draw out her feelings.

She blinked, opened her mouth to answer but no words emerged.

'I'm leaving tomorrow,' he pushed, needing to hear her declare herself before he walked away. 'I've been trying to give you space and not put pressure on the situation, because I've done that before and it didn't work out well for me. But I can't leave without at least raising the possibility of a relationship between us.'

She frowned, her eyes darting away and he had his answer. 'I'm not sure what you expect me to say to that, Conrad.' She dragged in a shaky breath. 'That I don't want you to leave tomorrow? That I *have* thought about us trying to have a real relationship?'

'Have you?' he asked, his chest tight. 'You haven't brought it up. Perhaps you were just going to wave goodbye without a backward glance.' Whereas he'd never felt more torn in two, even before the pregnancy scare.

'Of course I've thought about it, and I can't see how it could work,' she whispered, her stare imploring so he wanted to hold her. 'You live in Australia. Your family is there. James. And mine is here. With Zach to consider, I'm not free to just think about myself and my own wants.'

He knew all of that, but, for him, those reasons

weren't permanent obstacles. Unless it wasn't that she didn't want a relationship, she just didn't want *him*.

'You're still not over the last serious relationship you had,' she said, 'otherwise you'd have no doubts about what you want. You'd be able to forgive your brother and move on. But you're stuck, Conrad, and the worst part is that I can understand why, and I don't blame you.' She sagged, as if exhausted.

He'd nodded along as she'd spoken, unable to argue with a single word. He *did* have doubts, because he'd felt Zara slipping away. He *was* stuck, but he'd started to feel that he could move on. For Conrad, the many obstacles she'd just articulated perfectly had seemed, for a moment, surmountable. But only if they felt the same way about each other, which obviously wasn't the case.

'When I want something serious,' she went on, 'I need a man who is sure about me *and* about Zach. Even if you lived here, even if you'd worked through your betrayal and grief, that would still be a big commitment. This, us, began as nothing serious. Trying to turn it into something else just feels…too hard.' She looked up, her eyes shining with emotions but her chin raised resolutely. She'd made up her mind.

'I understand,' he said, his insides hollow. 'I've been trying to change the rules, I know that.' Because she'd changed *him*. She'd made him see that he could let go of the past. 'I just hoped you might want more than a good time.'

'I'm not sure what I want in terms of a relationship,' she went on, reaching for him and then thinking better of it, her hand falling to her lap. 'But I know I can't afford to make another mistake like last time. I have to put Zach first.'

'So I would be a mistake?' She put him in the same category as Zach's father. She didn't want him. Couldn't trust him. Wasn't willing to take a risk for him.

She shook her head violently. 'No, of course not. I don't know. This is the first time I've had to think about relationships since I became a mother. I'm just trying to do the right thing, for me and Zach, because I don't want either of us to be hurt.' She shook her head in defeat.

'It's okay, Zara. Maybe you're right—it *is* too hard. I'm leaving and I'm not making you any promises. I don't have all the answers. I just knew how I felt—that I'd do almost anything to try and make us work. But now there's no baby, I guess we don't have to worry about it.'

He stood, needing to get away. How could he have been so wrong about her? Yes, they both still struggled with trust, but while he'd been thinking of moving his entire life to be with her and Zach, to build a relationship with her, she'd been preparing to walk away, to push him away and keep her feelings safe.

'I'm sorry,' she said, sadly, looking up at him.

'So am I.' Conrad nodded, his stomach in knots. He wanted to throw out a glib comment like, *If you ever make it to Australia, give me a call.* But he'd never felt less like smiling.

'Take care, Zara,' he said instead. 'Of Zach and yourself.' And then he left.

CHAPTER EIGHTEEN

THE NEXT DAY, with her heart torn to shreds, Zara walked past the doctor's office on the postnatal ward and automatically glanced inside. Of course, there was no chance now of a clandestine glimpse of Conrad, just as there was no point hugging her secret close as she'd done every other day of their fling. It was over. He was gone. By the time she arrived home from her early shift, his flat would be empty and he'd be on the train to London for his evening flight to Brisbane. And it was for the best.

Seeing again his relieved expression when she'd confirmed there was no baby, Zara swallowed down the vicious pang of longing in her chest and shuffled towards the nurses' station. What had she expected? That he'd want to make a family with her and Zach? That he would move his entire life to be with them?

Their final conversation spun sickeningly in her mind. How had it gone so wrong at the end? And why, when it was always meant to be temporary, when he'd always planned to return to Australia, did she feel guilty and scared that she'd made a horrible mistake in refusing to talk about a future?

'Where's the new registrar?' Sharon said in an impatient voice as she shuffled items on the desk and then located a pen. 'I need them to prescribe some painkillers for the woman in bed ten.'

Zara shrugged, making some non-committal noise as she wiped two patient names from the whiteboard behind the desk. What did she care for the new registrar? The only thing that mattered was that the new doctor wouldn't be Conrad. She swallowed convulsively, her eyes stinging.

'What are you doing?' Sharon asked, snapping Zara's attention back to the present.

Zara looked up to see that she'd wiped the whiteboard clean of every name. Defeated and close to breaking down, she replaced the whiteboard eraser, her shoulders slumping. 'I'll write the names back up,' she muttered.

'I don't care about the names,' Sharon said, taking Zara's elbow and ushering her inside the vacant nurses' office, clearly sensing something was very wrong. 'What's going on with you today?' Sharon demanded, closing the door. 'Is it Zach?'

Mention of her son made things worse. Because she'd not only let Conrad down, let herself down because she was scared to admit the depth of her feelings, she'd also taken something from Zach. Her son didn't need a mother who moped around, living a half-life. And now that Conrad was gone, she saw so clearly how her fling with him had brought her back to life. But if she tried to explain the entire situation to her friend, she'd definitely break down, the well of emotion rising in her throat almost overwhelming.

'No, Zach is fine.' Zara shook her head, trying to reassure her friend that it was nothing serious. 'I just got distracted,' Zara said feebly.

'I'm not talking about the whiteboard.' Sharon fisted her hands on her hips. 'You look close to tears. I've never seen you cry.' Sharon urged Zara into a seat, taking the one opposite. 'It's Conrad, isn't it? You weren't just having sex— you've fallen in love with him, haven't you? And now he's going back to Australia.'

Zara spluttered, mortified. 'No! Don't be silly.' Although she'd come pretty close to falling. Why else would she feel so…bereft now that he'd left?

'Are you sure?' Sharon pressed, her expression somehow both stern and sympathetic. 'Because you've been walking around like a zombie all morning and the only change is that he's flying back to Australia later this evening.'

Feeling weak with hypoglycaemia—she had

zero appetite—Zara collapsed back into the chair. 'I told you: it was just sex, but obviously it's over now. I'll be fine. I'll get over it. I'm just…adjusting, that's all.'

But now that the 'L' word was out there, she couldn't ignore it. Could Sharon be right? Had she actually fallen deeply in love with Conrad? Could that explain the frantic panic making her desperate to rewind time and handle their final conversation differently? How stupid would she be if it were true? She wasn't having his baby, but Australia was even further away than Spain, and even if she was in love with him, Conrad could never love her back, could he…?

'How did he take the news about the test being negative?' Sharon asked, her voice cautious.

Zara shrugged. 'Fine, obviously. He was relieved.'

'Was he?' Sharon frowned. 'Are you sure?'

Zara looked up sharply. 'Of course he was. We were never in a relationship and he lives in Australia. Why? What do you know…?' Fear snaked down her spine.

'Nothing,' Sharon said, her expression serious. 'It's just that yesterday when I mentioned you were going to take a test, I thought he looked… excited for a second. But maybe I was wrong.'

Zara dropped her face into her hands, her mind reeling. She'd been so caught up in her own emotions—panic that she'd made another mistake, guilt that she'd told Sharon and hurt Conrad, fear that he'd reject her, just like Lorenzo, and she'd be devastated—that she'd taken Conrad's relief at face value. She'd told him a relationship with him would be too hard and as good as shoved him onto the plane.

But what if Sharon was right? What if he'd been trying to say he wanted a relationship and she'd finally and definitively pushed him away out of fear?

Closing her eyes, she saw his face as it had been last night, his expression flat with disappointment, his stare hollow with betrayal, because she'd not only let him down, she'd also clung to the safety of her independence and kept him out emotionally. How could she have been such a coward? He'd wanted to talk about the possibility of a relationship and she'd refused, dismissed him and the idea, let him believe she didn't want him enough, when, in truth, if Conrad wanted a real relationship with her, she'd move her and Zach to the ends of the earth for him.

With a sudden gasp, she looked up. It hit her like a blow. Sharon was right. She'd fallen in love with Conrad and she'd run scared from him and from her feelings. Why, in the cold light of day, with Conrad gone, did it now seem so obvious?

Seeing the moment of realisation on Zara's face, Sharon nodded and placed her hand on Zara's knee. 'What happened after you told him about the negative test?' she asked, her voice tinged with sickening sympathy that turned Zara's veins to ice.

'I told him I was scared to make another mistake. And then to make certain I'd killed it stone dead, when he wanted to talk about the possibility of a relationship between us, I pointed out that it was too hard and pushed him away.' She hung her head in shame.

Sharon said nothing, which was somehow worse than a stern lecture or an *I told you so.*

'Oh, no…' Zara moaned, feeling sick. 'I was so terrified of making a mistake again that I've actually gone and made the biggest one of my life, haven't I?' She looked up and lasered her friend with a stare, as if demanding a denial would fix it.

But just as they had with Lorenzo, her actions had consequences. Only this time, with Conrad, those consequences were more devastating. She was in love with a wonderful man she'd sent away without telling him of her feelings.

His words from the night before returned to haunt her.

I just knew how I felt—that I'd do almost anything to try and make us work.

He'd obviously been trying to tell her he wanted more. What if he *was* ready to have a serious relationship again and wanted one with her but she'd pushed him away because she'd still been scared to risk her heart? He wouldn't likely declare his feelings and move his whole life to England on the off chance that she might one day wake up and want to date him for real. Could he forgive her? Could he possibly love her back one day? Because now that she was thinking about it, she was pretty certain that was what she felt for Conrad. That over the past few weeks, despite every barrier she'd put up against it, she had fallen in love with him.

Sharon pressed her lips together in a stubborn line. 'Could you back up a bit? Call him and tell him you want to try and do long distance, maybe tell him how you feel about him? Maybe you could visit him in Australia and see how it goes?'

Zara shook her head. Would Conrad want to hear it? 'I think it's too late,' she said, tears threatening. She'd hurt Conrad because she was scared to hope for a real relationship. She'd convinced herself she just wanted sex, nothing serious, but Conrad had been right: she'd spent years punishing herself for the mistake of Lorenzo and denying herself romance and sex and love. And she'd found all of those things with Conrad.

'Even if he wasn't leaving tonight,' she went

on, 'neither of us has been in a serious relationship for years. What if he won't give me a second chance?' Conrad had so much to work through—forgiving Marcus, reuniting with James and reconciling with Tessa, looking for a consultant job. But now that she'd woken up to the fact that she was in love with him, that serious relationship she'd put off for so long while she punished herself and lived in fear was suddenly the *only* thing she wanted.

'That sounds like the old Zara talking,' Sharon said softly. 'The one who seemed to be going through the motions of her life, not needing anyone else. The one whose smile was rare. If I'm honest, that Zara was a bit uptight.' Sharon smiled apologetically and reached for Zara's hand. 'You've come alive this past month.'

Zara nodded, her smile wobbling and her eyes smarting with tears. 'I know. It's him.'

'It's the two of you together,' Sharon stated. 'You complement each other. That's when the magic happens, when sex and connection turn into love.'

Zara sniffed, trying to pull herself together. They were at work, after all. And just because she loved him, didn't mean he had the same feelings for her. Could he want her and Zach? Because they came as a pair. She needed to apologise for running scared and find out.

Suddenly energised, Zara stood. 'I'll call him when my shift ends. Before he gets on that plane.' She glanced at the watch pinned to her uniform for the time. She could tell him how stupid she'd been. Confess that she had feelings for him and ask if there was any way they could make a real, serious relationship work. No more secrets. Should she also tell him she was in love with him? Or would he think that was too much, too soon?

'There's the Zara I've wanted to see all these years,' Sharon said with a smile of encouragement. 'We're quiet today and overstaffed. Why don't you finish up early? Call him now? I'll cover you.'

'Really?' Zara asked, her eyes filling with tears.

'Of course,' Sharon said. 'I've been rooting for you to find someone for years. Don't keep me hanging. Go.'

'Thanks. I'll let you know how it goes.' Throwing her arms around Sharon, Zara rushed to the doctor's office, where she'd left her bag, coat and phone.

CHAPTER NINETEEN

FROM THE DERBY to London train, Conrad opened his emails in an attempt to forget about the devastating final conversation he'd had with Zara. Last night, after leaving Zara's place, he'd messaged his parents to tell them he'd be leaving as planned and would see them soon. Until that very moment, he'd agonised over the decision of whether to leave or stay. But what was the point in delaying his departure from the UK when Zara had made it clear that she'd had her fun and that their fling was over?

Hollowness built inside him at the memories of their fight. Not that they'd raised their voices. It had been more of a quiet acceptance that they'd finally arrived at the end of their journey. Only for him, it hadn't been over. Before they'd become distracted by the possibility of a pregnancy and by Zara's explanations about Sharon, he'd wanted to force Zara's hand. To confront her with the idea of them seeing each other again, either in England, or Australia.

But he'd soon realised there'd been no sense pushing it; she didn't want *him*. She was scared to risk her heart, scared to make a mistake, scared to expose Zach to a man who might not stick around. And Conrad couldn't blame her. It wasn't as if he even lived in the UK. Not only did Zara have to think about Zach, just as Conrad needed to look out for James, but their situation was also complicated by a whole world of distance.

With a sigh of inevitability, and to distract himself from the pain gnawing a hole in his chest, Conrad opened the email reply from his mother. He scanned the message, reaching the last paragraph.

In other news, Tessa called. It seems she's turned a bit of a corner and is feeling up to being more social. She brought James to visit yesterday, asked about your travels and then asked if Dad and I can help out with school pickups when she goes back to work...

Conrad tried to focus on the words his mother had written, but the news didn't fill him with the relief he'd imagined. He was happy for his parents, for Tessa, for James. Families needed to pull together, especially in times of grief. But as something shifted from Conrad's shoulders, a weight he hadn't known he'd carried easing, he realised with a start that the mess he'd run away from wasn't his responsibility. Maybe because ever since the night he'd told Zara about Marcus's betrayal, he'd also started talking to his brother in his head. He'd taken Zara's advice and begun to properly work through forgiving Marcus. He still had much grieving to do, of course. But that was no reason for him to be alone, to pass by a relationship with an amazing woman who'd brought *him* back to life.

Zara had been right—he *had* been stuck and hiding from his feelings. She'd helped him to see that he was still clinging to that sense of betrayal, because he was scared to let anyone close again or to fall in love. Scared that he'd lose another person he cared about or be betrayed or rejected. Only he hadn't been able to keep Zara out. She'd found a way under his guard anyway.

But at the first sign of trouble, he'd run again. He'd allowed her to push him away when he'd wanted to fight for them, to tell her his feelings and how he wanted a serious relationship. How he wanted her *and* Zach.

Sending a hurried reply to his mother, Conrad fought his rising sense of panic. Life was too short for regrets. He might have said that a hundred times, but it was only with Zara that he'd truly believed it. He saw now, with crystal clarity, that he'd been going through the motions before he'd met Zara. He'd called her out on hiding behind the mistake she'd made, on punishing herself, when he'd been hiding too. For all his talk of embracing the good times, the best times he'd had in years had been with Zara. Only a complete idiot would walk away from that before making sure there was no way in hell he could make it work.

Zara's reproach resounded in his head, as if she were in the train carriage with him, hurtling towards London.

I'm not sure what you expect me to say to that, Conrad. That I don't want you to leave...? That I have thought about us trying to have a real relationship?

Did that mean that if he lived in England, or if she lived in Australia, she'd want a serious relationship with him? Didn't he owe it to himself, to them both, to find out? Now!

Fresh panic seized him by the throat. He couldn't leave England like this, sloping off with his tail between his legs, scared to tell her that he wanted more than a fling. Scared to know if she wanted the same. He wasn't ready to give up on them just because they had commitments and lived in different countries. There must be a way to make something so good work. He'd move heaven and earth to enable them to be together if that was what she wanted. But first, he had to tell her what *he* wanted.

With his mind working properly for the first time in what felt like days, he typed a few extra lines to his mother.

Change of plan this end. Might not make flight today after all. Will keep you posted.

He pressed send, jerked to his feet and grabbed his bag. Then, manhandling his suitcase from the luggage rack, he positioned himself in the exit, so when the train stopped at the next station, he could get off and swap platforms.

His heart galloped with yearning and possibility. It wasn't over, not when he'd neglected to tell her that his feelings for her were no longer casual or *nothing serious*. And he needed to do that in person. Zara was at work. She wouldn't answer her phone if he called. There was only one way to make her understand how he felt about her and that was to head back to Derby.

CHAPTER TWENTY

WITH HER HEART THUNDERING, Zara ducked into the doctor's office on the postnatal ward and fished her phone out of her bag. With trembling fingers, she held her breath as the phone powered on, willing time to stand still or go backwards so she could make this right. What if he couldn't wait to get back to the Sunshine Coast, where he would easily forget about her and their brief fling? What if he got on the plane before she could tell him she was sorry and that she loved him? What if she missed her chance to be happy because she'd made the massive mistake of pushing him away?

With her veins full of icy panic, the screen of her phone lit up. She was just about to unlock it and dial Conrad, when several alert sounds came in, one after another.

Ping, ping, ping.

She opened the most recent text, elated to see it was from Conrad.

Phone low on charge. Can't call again but we need to talk.

Zara sagged with relief. He wanted to talk. That sounded promising. Seeing she also had three voicemails from him, she grabbed her coat and bag and put the phone to her ear so she could listen to the message as she walked to the car. Hopefully Conrad would have recharged his phone somewhere by the time she called him back.

She'd just stepped from the office, his voicemail playing in her ear—'Zara, we need to talk...'—when she looked up to find Conrad striding down the ward towards her pulling his suitcase.

Dropping the phone to her side, she gaped at the wonderful sight of him in person. 'What are you doing here?' she said, her throat raw with longing, her mind foggy with confusion. 'Did you miss your flight?'

He shook his head, dropped his bags to the floor and cupped her face between both his palms. Then his lips covered hers and he dragged her into his arms.

Zara dropped everything, including her phone, which clattered to the floor with its voicemail from Conrad still playing. She tunnelled her fingers into his hair and parted her lips, kissing him back with everything she had, as if it were her last chance ever. She was too high to care that the other midwives might see, not to mention the patients. He was here. He wanted to talk. He was kissing her. Nothing else mattered.

She clung to him, yelping in protest when he tore his mouth from hers. 'I need to talk to you,' he said, panting hard, his stare flicking wildly between her eyes.

She nodded, dragging him into the doctor's office and closing the door, her hand in his. 'Conrad, I'm so sorry about last night,' she said, launching into her apology. 'Are you okay? What happened?' She swept her gaze over him, still doubting he was real.

Conrad shook his head. 'I'm fine. I got off the train. I came back to tell you I've figured everything out,' he said, gripping her hand as if he'd never let her go. 'I'm in love with you, Zara.'

Zara frowned, her heart clenching with wild longing. His words made no sense. Had she heard him right? He loved her?

'I realised it on the platform in Kettering,' he went on, scrubbing a hand through his hair. 'Wherever the hell that is.'

Despite the confusion and euphoria ransacking her body, Zara laughed and Conrad cupped her face with an indulgent smile.

'I was sitting on the train,' he rushed on, 'and

I realised that I'd run away again, without telling you how I feel about you.'

'Me too,' she cried, gripping him tighter. 'I'm so sorry that I pushed you away. That I made you doubt. I want you to know that I *do* trust you. That you could never be a mistake. That I don't care how hard it is, I want to make us work.'

He cut her off with another kiss. 'I know you're scared,' he said when he pulled back, 'and I am too. But I love you, harder than I've ever been in love before.'

She tried to interject but he shook his head and continued. 'You were right about me. I *was* hiding from the past, running away from it, shielding myself with casual relationships so I didn't have to face the risk of anyone else betraying me or finding out that no one could ever love me. But my fear isn't enough of a reason to walk away from you, from the most real relationship I've ever had. I want you, Zara. You *and* Zach.'

'Conrad,' she said, trying to get a word in, to tell him that *she* loved him, too, but he rushed on.

'I'm ready to let go of the past, Zara, and actually build a real, serious relationship with you, if you'll let me.'

'Conrad, I want that, too. But what about your job in Australia? Your family? James?' Tears stung Zara's eyes, his words were so wonderful, but she'd still have to let him go, at least in the short term.

'Yes.' He nodded, his stare softening. 'I still need to address all of that, but that shouldn't stop us being together. I don't know how exactly—I'll move here, or you and Zach can come to Brisbane or we'll alternate. The point is, I want to be with you. I love you, Zara. That's what I want—us. You, me and Zach. But…what do you want?'

Zara laughed, her tears finally spilling free. 'Well, if you'd let me get a word in, I'd have told you that I want to be with you too. That's why I was leaving early just now, to call you and tell you how I feel. I didn't want you to get in the plane without knowing.' She looked down from the joy sparkling in his beautiful eyes, ashamed. 'I'm so sorry about last night. The way I pushed you away.' She looked up and met his stare. 'You're right: I was scared. Terrified, actually. For a moment, I thought history was repeating itself with that pregnancy scare. I thought you could never love me. Never want me and Zach. But this, with you, has been the first real, grown-up relationship I've ever had.'

'I know it's moving crazy fast.' Conrad frowned, his stare so intense, she gasped. 'But we owe it to ourselves to see where this could go. I know you're scared to make another mistake, but I won't let you down, Zara. You or Zach.'

She nodded. 'I know you won't. And it's *not* too fast. I've waited six years for this, for *you*. We could never be a mistake, because I finally know now what love truly feels like. Real, grown-up love. I love you too, Conrad.'

His brows pinched together as hope bloomed in his eyes. 'You do?'

'Yes.' Zara laughed, cried, threw her arms around his neck and pressed her lips to his stunned mouth. 'I didn't properly realise it until today when Sharon helpfully pointed it out. But somewhere along my wild sexual adventure, I fell in love with you. I think it might have been when I watched you build your first snowman.'

Conrad grinned, kissed her and then pulled back, falling serious. 'About Zach. I know he's your top priority, but I want you to know that I love him too, because he's yours. I want to help you raise him and one day, when you're ready, I want him to be *ours*.'

Zara blinked, her throat aching. 'You are so wonderful.' Joy burst past her lips in a wave of laughter he kissed up as he wiped the tears from her cheeks.

They stared at each other with goofy grins on their faces for so long, Zara felt guilty for hogging the office. 'What shall we do now?' she asked, her hands caressing his face as if committing him to memory, knowing that she couldn't keep him, because he still needed to go back to Australia. 'Can you still make your flight?'

She would miss him. But she was already planning to apply for some annual leave so she could take Zach to visit him in Brisbane.

'There's more snow due, apparently,' Conrad said, drawing her into his arms once more. 'I saw it on the news before my phone died. If you'll have me, I'll come home with you tonight and take another flight to Brisbane in a few days.'

She smiled. 'I think that could be arranged. You can't fly anywhere if you're snowed in, maybe even trapped in my bed.'

His smile widened, his stare loaded with sensual promise. 'How soon before you could visit me in Australia? I need to tie up loose ends back home, to see James and my parents, but then I want to come back here, to be with you. To make this work. This time our relationship will be out in the open and *very* serious, so I hope you're prepared.'

Zara smiled, laughed, pressed her lips to his. 'I'll only come to Australia if you promise me a tour of the Sunshine Coast. It's been a long time since I've worn a bikini.'

'I think that could be arranged,' he replied, throwing her words back at her. Then he dragged her close for another deep and passionate kiss.

Neither of them noticed the office door being

pushed open or Sharon stepping aside so anyone within peering distance could see them kiss. It was only when the applause and cheering started that Zara broke away from Conrad, and they turned, blushing to see their audience of teary-eyed midwives and mums cradling their new babies.

'Let's get out of here,' Zara said to Conrad, once her laughter had died down. 'We can pick up Zach from school and make plans for our visit to Australia. He'll be so excited.'

Conrad reached for her hand and they left the ward to more whoops and cheering, the loudest from Sharon, who yelled, 'Go get him, Zara.'

Zara met Conrad's beaming stare, her heart ready to explode. 'I fully intend to,' she said, slinging her arm around his waist.

He pressed a kiss to her lips, smiled that killer smile and winked. 'I'm all yours.'

EPILOGUE

One year later

THAT JANUARY IN BRISBANE, summer temperatures reached record highs. So the only sensible place for a wedding was on the beach. North of Brisbane, on a white sand cove on the island of K'gari, Zara and Conrad stood under a white linen awning, making their vows before a small gathering of friends and family.

Zara curled her bare toes into the sand and gripped Conrad's hands tighter in hers, certain that for the rest of her life, she'd hold him close—her best friend, her lover, her husband. Love and passion and devotion shone from his grey eyes, all but melting the simple strapless wedding dress she wore clean off. She couldn't wait to get him alone, couldn't wait to start this new adventure with him: their marriage. But first, she planned to enjoy every second of their wedding day.

'As Zara and Conrad have exchanged their

vows of togetherness and exchanged rings, symbols of for ever,' their wedding celebrant said to their small congregation of guests, which included Pam, Zara's mother, and Sharon and Rod, who'd also made the journey, 'they move forward, their lives entwined as husband and wife and as parents to Zach.'

Their loved ones cheered and clapped as Zara surged up on tiptoes, her lips clashing with Conrad's in their first kiss as husband and wife. As always, she lost herself to their chemistry, holding him tight, kissing him hard, laughing against his smile, because falling in love with Conrad Reed had brought her endless joy.

'I love you,' he said, pulling back to peer down at her with desire and something close to adoration. And the feelings were very much reciprocated.

'I love you too,' she said, laughing through her tears as she reflected on the past year, where they'd bounced around between Australia and England, finally settling in Brisbane where they now worked in the same hospital.

Her lips found his once more and everything slotted perfectly into place. But she could only enjoy kissing her new husband for a few seconds, as two little boys, their two ring-bearers, Zach and James, pulled them apart with embarrassed squeals.

Conrad laughed, his hands resting on Zach's and James's shoulders. Zara's heart burst with love for him. He was such an amazing father and uncle, and the boys had become close friends.

As their guests surged forward to offer congratulations, hugs and kisses, Zara counted herself the luckiest woman alive. She had everything she could possibly want.

'Congratulations,' Sharon said as she hugged Zara close. 'I told you that you needed to live a little, have a little fun, didn't I? And look how it all turned out.'

Zara laughed at her smug friend, her stare meeting Conrad's. 'You're right. It's been the best time of my life.' Not that she regretted a single second of the journey that had brought her to Conrad, the man she loved.

Later, after photos on the beach, her husband snagged her hand and held her back as their guests wandered back to the lodge where their wedding party would take place.

Stepping into his arms, she raised her lips to his kiss. He cupped her face, that secret smile in his eyes as he peered down at her. 'Any regrets?' he asked playfully, secure in her love because she showed him what he meant to her every day.

'Just one,' she said, slipping her hands around his waist. 'Our celebrations are going to be way too long. I have to wait hours before I can get my hands on all this.' She slid her palms up his chest, over his white linen shirt, caressing his defined pecs.

'I know what you mean,' he said, his stare full of sensual promise as he gave her body a heated glance. 'But that's what a honeymoon is for. I love the boys, dearly,' he said about James and Zach, 'but I can't wait to have you all to myself for an entire week. Brace yourself for another wild sexual adventure, Mrs Reed.' He grinned and brushed her lips with his.

Zara melted into his arms, grateful to Conrad's parents, who would watch Zach for the week they'd be away in Fiji.

'So you think you're the man for the job, do you?' she teased, sighing into another kiss. She wasn't going to be able to keep her hands or her lips off him today.

Playfully, he cracked his knuckles. 'I'll certainly give it my best shot.'

They smiled, kissed again, this one turning heated enough to make Zara's breath catch.

'Mum…stop kissing,' Zach called from across the beach.

Zara and Conrad laughed and headed after their friends and family, arm in arm. 'I'm not sure I can make that promise,' she said, looking up at the love of her life.

'Me neither,' Conrad said, pausing to press his lips to hers. 'But I can promise that I'll always love you.'

'Me too.'

* * * * *

*If you enjoyed this story, check out
these other great reads from
JC Harroway*

Forbidden Fiji Nights with Her Rival
Secretly Dating the Baby Doc
Nurse's Secret Royal Fling
Her Secret Valentine's Baby

All available now!